McAlister's Lady

By

Richard Marman

Cover image by Michael Marman
Other graphics and design by Richard Marman

The McAlister Line

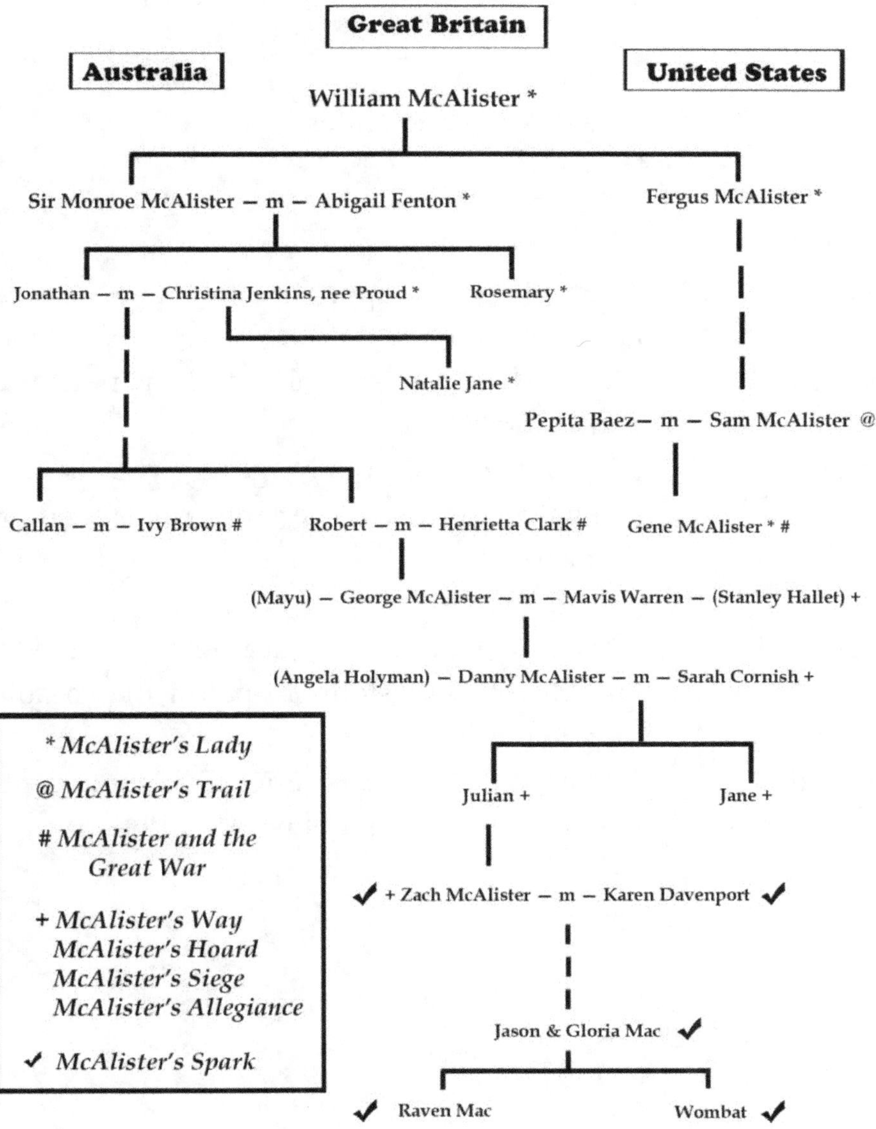

Glossary and Notes

Cable	Nautical length approximately one hundred and eighty metres
Exploring Officers	Mounted officers sent ahead of main army to gather intelligence
Landers	18th and 19th Century agents who handled smuggled goods once they're landed on English soil
Owlers	Smugglers
Riding Officers	18th and 19th Century night-riders appointed by His Majesty's Customs to patrol the coastline for smugglers
Venturers	18th and 19th Century English landed gentry who invested in smuggling operations

Prologue — Merimbula NSW

Hi there. If you've got around to reading this then you'll probably know I'm Zach McAlister and I have been researching my family history along with my Grandpa Danny and his girlfriend, Angela Holyman. Initially the stories were about Danny and Angela's adventures in the 1950s, so we were able to rely on their memories which were as sharp as steel traps, but we also discovered some interesting tit-bits about other McAlisters.

Angela is a whiz-kid when it comes to research and it's amazing what she can uncover when she delves beyond Wikipedia way down into scholastic data-bases where only mega-nerds dare go. She also knows egg-heads in a squillion universities, libraries, museums and can access council and church records all over the world. And we found a considerable number of personal journals and family correspondence to supplement our investigations.

Some of the information is widely documented while other stories have been pieced together from snippets almost hidden in antiquity. We also found many historical black-holes where the events are pure speculation.

Angela's mum did most of the heavy-lifting when it came to early collation of this story. I alluded to it in *McAlister's Allegiance,* so now you'll get to know the whole story...well most of it anyway.

McAlister's Lady

Chapter 1 — Shipwreck

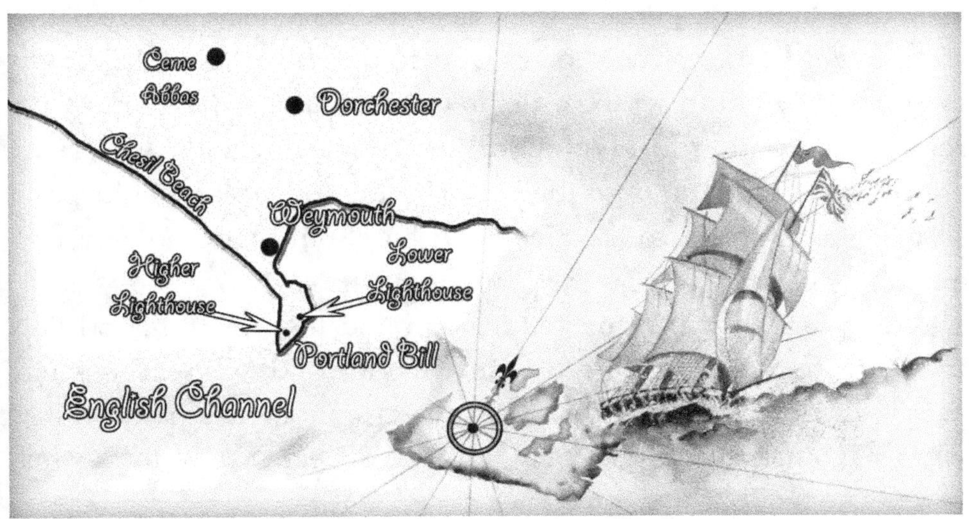

Will Jenkins was born on the Dorset Coast and decided to follow in his father's footsteps by becoming a smugglers' lander. Old Wally Jenkins was a smith by trade and while he trained his son as an apprentice, both man and boy felt that contraband brandy, silk and spices were far quicker ways of earning a few extra sovereigns.

Well not a few actually — many.

In the first decade of the nineteenth century there was gold aplenty for anyone with skill and daring enough to run the Royal Navy blockade from France and dodge the excise cutters prowling England's southern ports.

Young Will was about eighteen at the time and something of a ladies' man. He was always ready to present a prettily embroidered handkerchief or charming nosegay to any coy maid who took his fancy. One such not-so-coy miss was sixteen-year-old

Christina Proud, the only daughter of Cornelius Proud and his goodwife, Emma.

The Reverend Proud was vicar of St Mary's Church, the spiritual heart of Cerne Abbas, a pretty village about half way between Weymouth on the coast and Yeovil along the main coach road from London to Plymouth. Now Reverend and Mrs Proud were what might be described as a 'robust' couple, who'd been suitably pious prior to their wedded bliss, but made no secret of exploiting God's gifts once respectably wed.

But for all their effusive affection and lust for the good life, the Prouds were only blessed with a single child, who grew into a pretty, cheerful, hardworking, warm-hearted if occasionally willful young woman. Christina may not have been as pious as her parents hoped, but they loved her none the less.

Pretty warm-hearted lasses were Will Jenkins' forte and on many occasions, he and Christina had been observed emerging from one village barn or another in a flushed and ruffled condition, leaving a trail of hay in their wake.

When Will finished his apprenticeship, which he'd started at ten years old, he became a journeyman in his father's forge until he'd either start his own business elsewhere or inherit the Cerne Abba smithy when Wally could no longer manage it. As a journeyman, Will was now entitled to wages, which he'd need to support a wife and potential family.

It was high time for Reverend Proud to call upon Master Smith Wally Jenkins and make some domestic arrangements. As the two Cerne Abbas worthies sat by Wally's snug hearth, they refilled their clay pipes and poured a second brandy of known-but-unacknowledged provenance. Their conversation went something like this…

'You know I have given some thought to our Christina and your Will,' Reverend Proud opened the bidding.

'Aye?'

As a smuggler, Wally wasn't in any hurry to give anything away.

'Indeed. The thing is the whole village knows they are sweethearts.'

'True enough.'

'They make a handsome couple and no doubt about that,' Reverend Proud persisted.

'Trouble be that our Will is sweet on most lasses within a day's ride. More for all I know.'

'I believe Christina will keep him fully occupied.'

'Maybe, but Will is also in what might be described as a high-risk occupation.'

'Well I know the forge has hazards, but no more than driving the mail coach — what with the pitiful state of the roads, bad weather, highwaymen and ...'

'No, Vicar. I'm thinkin' more of 'is night-work...'

'Not a word more, Wally,' Proud protested. 'You understand I am a law-abiding citizen with no knowledge of dishonesty in my parish.'

'I daresay, Vicar,' Wally eyed his guest slyly, 'but I know you are well-stocked with fine port wine and brandy spirit which I have been able to supply from a confidential source — a supply I'm sure you have no wish to dry up.'

'Quite so, quite so. There is nothing in God's sacred word that forbids a man enjoying His bountiful gifts. Does not Chapter 2 of the Holy Gospel according to our blessed Saint John state our Lord Jesus Himself turned water into wine? To keep the party going so to speak — not to mention saving the father-of-the-bride's reputation.'

'Just as long as we are clear that the supplier will continue to…supply.'

Reverend Proud nodded.

'Whatever the risks to himself and his…kinfolk.'

The prospect of Reverend Proud's future son-in-law being an owler wasn't really an issue for the good cleric. Excise taxes had risen steadily all Proud's life and what was the money for? A never ending war — that's what! It was 1809. British and Portuguese forces opposed Marshal Soul's French legions advancing from Spain — a fight that had degenerated into bloody stalemate.

Less than a month ago in January British commander, Sir John Moore, was killed at the Battle of Corunna. One of Moore's talented subordinates, Lieutenant General Sir Arthur Wellesley had been appointed to resume the struggle against Bonaparte's hordes on the Iberian Peninsula. Yet the French had been victorious everywhere in Spain and Wellesley must march his army across treacherous and hostile terrain if he was to give the Corsican upstart's villains the sound thrashing they deserved.

Reverend Proud also noticed that while the Exchequer's coffers poured endless funds into the war-effort, it spent precious little on those returned warriors so badly maimed they were reduced to beggary. Every village or town in Britain had their share of men so physically and mentally scarred they relied on parish charity. The Dorset Yeomanry and militia regiments were no exception.

Less tax paid meant more for the offertory with returned soldiers and sailors being top priority in Proud's view. The bishop disagreed, feeling church glory was better symbolised by the fine trappings of High Anglican edifices in the diocese. Emma Proud utilised much creative book-keeping to keep his grace off the scent.

So the deal was struck and the wedding planned for Christina's seventeenth birthday.

Christina kept a diary and penned entries almost daily. She recorded she was thrilled and could hardly wait for the upcoming nuptials. Why not, she was betrothed to the most dashing handsome and eligible fellow in the county? Being just seventeen on her wedding day wasn't unusual for the time. It was far better to be wed young than wind up pregnant, abandoned and on the way to the workhouse. And in truth the potential groom-pool bar wasn't set especially high in bucolic Pre-Regency England. How Will felt remained unrecorded.

So the marriage proceeded without a hitch and of course the bride looked stunning in a fine white dress complemented by a crown of early spring-flowers upon her head. The wedding breakfast was a feast remembered by townsfolk long afterwards.

And that would have been that. Christina joined the Jenkins' household to settle down, dutifully produce a family and grow into a contented, plump country goodwife. But although Will didn't consciously have other ideas, fate intervened and Christina's life took a completely different path…

*

There were advantages and drawbacks to smuggling as the days lengthened. On the plus side the weather was generally fair and the sea calmer. However long balmy twilights made the window of opportunity to import cargoes much shorter and the tidal movement became far more critical. And tides, especially the notorious Portland Race, could be a trial for even seasoned mariners along England's south coast.

As a lander, Will's job was to organize transport and teamsters for the cargo, store the contraband before finally distribution to waiting customers. He was then responsible for seeing the venturers received their profits and all hands paid off either in coin or merchandise.

Will wasn't without rivals, although the main competition came from a gang of toughs led by a Weymouth lay-about called Toff Fleming. Toff's men supplemented their income by waylaying drunks from dock-side taverns and selling them to Royal Navy press-gangs in exchange for a few guineas and immunity from naval service themselves.

But Toff wasn't averse to scavenging. He was a wrecker, although there was nothing unusual about that. Every coastal community kept a weather-eye out for shipping in distress — and there was plenty about along that treacherous shoreline.

A wreck normally spewed any amount of valuable flotsam, which was deemed legitimate salvage. Folk hurried to any accessible beach to gather whatever they could scrounge. Many would sail or row to sea in small boats to retrieve cargo still afloat and they even rescued survivors.

Another individual involved in the incident about to change Will and Christina's lives irrevocably was newly appointed district Sheriff Nathaniel Lightfoot. He was a dour man of Puritan descent and eager to see the west-country rid of all forms of vice, especially illegal booze. To that end he had selected four of the Weymouth Customs House's most reliable riding-officers to patrol the cliff-tops for nefarious activity. Finding four good men and true hadn't been easy among the ill-paid night-riders who were generally susceptible to bribery, if not in league with the smuggling gangs themselves.

That volatile mix of personalities was to collide one night in late March or early April — dates vary — but the events were widely documented in news-sheets and official accounts…

*

A tri-master East Indiaman, *Lady Annabelle* beat its way along the Dorset coast bound for Southampton. She was returning from a two-year voyage to China, Dutch Indonesia and the sub-continent with her holds crammed with Eastern silks, spices and opium — for medicinal use of course. Her master was in a hurry and eager to get home.

At the same time the brig *Sea-Snake* streaked towards its secret destination close to Weymouth taking advantage of the incoming tide. *Sea-Snake's* cargo was French cognac, cheese, claret and perfume, Italian silk, lace and baskets of early season peaches.

Sea-Snake's manifest was not public knowledge and kept safely tucked inside the boot of her master, a bearded, swashbuckling seafarer known in smuggling circles as Dandy-Jim Mullins. He'd made countless channel crossings and was just the fellow to find if you wanted the job done. Both French and English spies relied on Dandy-Jim's impartiality and discretion, paying handsomely for their passages.

At three bells into the first watch, as evening drew into night, Dandy-Jim manoeuvred his craft with expert skill assisted by local knowledge. The twinkling beacon of the lower and higher lighthouses declared Portland Bill, a notorious shipping hazard, littered with wrecks over the centuries. The East Indiaman's master was not so well informed, and right then the twin lights on Portland Bill snuffed out.

'What the deuce..?' Dandy-Jim muttered.

'Sail on the larboard bow!' *Sea-Snake's* forward lookout yelled. 'Two cables away, skipper and bearing straight down on us.'

The giant vessel had appeared from nowhere, looming above *Sea-Snake's* deck like an evil spectre of doom

'Hard a-starboard,' Dandy-Jim ordered the helmsman standing at his side. The skipper neither raised his voice nor gave a hint of alarm. 'All hands to the sheets, sharply now if you please, Thomas,' he added, addressing his first mate.

And so it was. The helmsman and two mates rammed the tiller fully starboard while Dandy-Jim issued orders to bring the brig around. As the sails luffed, flapping languidly, *Sea-Snake* lost way while the East Indiaman crashed through the surf towards her.

But Dandy-Jim judged his position perfectly. As the bowsprit swung to the right, the wind bit into the sails and *Sea-Snake* surged away just as the monster ship swept past, leaving the smugglers' brig rocking in her wake.

'What the devil are they playing at?' Thomas demanded once the danger was past and they'd re-trimmed *Sea-Snake's* sails.

'Lookee, skipper,' a lookout called, 'she's headed fer the Bill. She'll founder f'sure on that tack. What 'appened to the lights?'

Without the Portland Bill lighthouses, the East Indiaman was in dire straits. She was driven relentlessly ashore by a brisk south-westerly and incoming tide with no guidance at all. Dandy-Jim on the other hand had made the channel crossing so many times he knew exactly where he was heading.

'She's tryin' ter tack fer Weymouth 'Arbour,' Thomas remarked. 'But she ain't got time. She'll be on the Shambles true enough.'

At first it seemed he was right, but there were other perils along that treacherous coast. The silhouetted *Lady Annabelle* floundered as she tried to steer clear of the Bill, but the wind left her sails slack as the grand vessel lost headway and drifted impotently with the current. There she wallowed for a few moments before the Portland Race struck.

The Race was a rip-current, which charged back and forth along the coast, sweeping the unwary where it pleased. *Lady Annabelle* was dragged westwards while *Sea-Snake* steered a parallel course, but with enough sea room to safely avoid the rocky Bill cliffs and the Shambles reef.

And for a time it appeared the East Indiaman would scrape past the Bill, but not quite. Her hull slammed into an underwater outcrop, ripping a gash in her side and shredding a dozen planks to splinters. Water poured through the wound at a fatal rate. The lower decks were swamped in minutes, trapping screaming crew and passengers alike. The cries wailed from below, only to be silenced when seawater smothered the victims.

The force of such a large ship was immense. The main mast snapped and tumbled overboard, dragging sails and rigging with it. *Sea-Snake's* crew heard cracking timbers as life was squeezed from *Lady Annabelle*.

'She's doomed,' Dandy-Jim muttered.

Yet still the East Indiaman floated although low in the water, battered by waves washing above its gunwales. The ship may have been better foundering on the Bill, wedged between the rocks where rescuers might reach her. But she swung abruptly and drifted towards Chesil Cove where she ground to a halt on the pebble ridges formed by tides and swell.

She was now close to shore, which might have seemed a God-send to the survivors who'd managed to clamber into the night air and now swarmed over *Lady Annabelle's* main deck. For some the temptation to leap overboard and make for shore was overwhelming.

Unfortunately the ship drew over three fathoms of draft, so several folk dropped into the sea never to surface. Others struggled to shore, only to be swept back to sea by breakers that pounded the pebble shore rolling the shingle into underwater coils forming a lethal rip-tide. It was a phenomenon well known to Chesil locals, who treated the beach with respect, avoiding the shoreline at all cost.

So *Lady Annabelle* wallowed haplessly in Chesil Cove. Surf battered her hull continuously to a point where the ship was in danger of disintegrating at any time.

Chapter 2 — No Good Deed Goes Unpunished

Along with *Sea-Snake's* crew, a number of other people witnessed the stricken wreck and Will Jenkins was among them. As a lander, he and his ten-man team waited for *Sea-Snake's* arrival. He positioned himself off the Bill's southern cliffs waiting for a lantern signal from Dandy-Jim indicating which one of several landing spots he chose to anchor depending on tide and sea condition. After counting the number of flashes from the brig, Will and his men would hurry along the shore to the rendezvous.

However Will was unaware that Toff Fleming also had an interest on the Dorset Coast that night. Toff was most likely ignorant of *Sea-Snake's* approach, but he certainly knew about the

East Indiaman. A couple of Toff's lookouts had spied the *Lady Annabelle,* decided she was making poor headway and might have trouble navigating past Portland Bill. They mounted up and galloped into Weymouth to tell their boss of potential pickings.

Toff lost no time gathering his gang with the intention of helping L*ady Annabelle* to her fate in mind. Will's landers and Toff's likely-lads must have arrived on Portland Bill within minutes of each other, but were blithely unaware of the fact as the moon had only just risen and was yet to illuminate events. Indeed Will didn't even know about L*ady Annabelle* and was only interested in *Sea-Snake's* arrival.

Toff split his Dorset toughs into two groups. One bunch headed for the lower lighthouse and the other to the higher lighthouse. A tap on the temple with a bailing-pin silenced the keepers before Toff's lads rounded up their families. They were bundled into storerooms at pistol-point and locked inside. The thugs then clambered up the steps to extinguish the Argand lamps illuminating through William Hutchison reflectors.

As the moon rose *Lady Annabelle's* drama unfolded. Will, who was essentially a good-hearted soul, forgot about the inbound contraband and turned his attention to the stricken East Indiaman.

'We cannot help on the shingle,' he cried to his companions. 'It's just too treacherous. We must alert Weymouth folk and see if we can find any rescue boats. Who's with me?'

'What about the lights?' one of Will's men asked.

'Good thought. Stephen, get into town and raise the alarm. Everyone else with me and we'll discover what devilry is afoot.'

On reaching the higher lighthouse, they discovered the keeper and his family bound and gagged in the kitchen.

'Masked men attacked us,' the keeper declared once he was free. 'They was masked and scared the wits outa me missus and nippers...and blimey, me 'ead 'urts like the devil.'

'No chance of guessing who they were..?'

'Can't say, but you'll find out on Chesil Beach, cos that's where they said they was headin'.'

'We had better get after them,' Will said, abandoning his initial caution regarding Chesil Beach's treacherous shingle.

'I must relight the Argand,' the keeper said.

'Right, can you send someone to the lower light? I'll wager the keeper over there has met the same fate.'

But that turned out to be unnecessary, because at that moment the lower lighthouse lamp illuminated.

'The keeper must have freed himself,' Will said as he and his landers dashed across Portland Bill to Chesil Beach guided by torch and moonlight.

When he reached the cliff tops overlooking Chesil Bay, Will was met by a scene of chaos. Dozens of torches and lanterns flickered below him, moving like darting fireflies. Will and his men scrambled down a well worn path to the beach and discovered Toff Fleming's gang was already there and busy.

Folk from nearby fishing huts also joined the scavengers and more people streamed towards the beach as the news of *Lady Annabelle's* fate spread.

The East Indiaman was only a quarter-mile from shore, rocking violently with every wave that pounded her. Cargo was already being tossed ashore from holes ripped into the holds. Groups of people tried to gather anything that landed, but they were hampered by the shifting pebbles and knew well enough not to venture into the shore breakers, fearing they'd be sucked under and swept to sea by the rip-tide.

By now the scene was bathed in moonlight and Will saw *Sea-Snake* beyond *Lady Annabelle*. He assumed Dandy-Jim — ever the opportunist —was salvaging cargo, but he hoped the smugglers were also rescuing any survivors they came across. Will then noticed a series of three lantern flashes winking from the brig every few seconds. This was the signal to rendezvous at Ringstead Bay just east of Osmington Mills, a hamlet not far from Weymouth. It meant crossing reefs, but Dandy-Jim knew the coast and must have deemed it the best anchorage.

Meanwhile several scuffles broke out over any beached cargo and Will recognised Toff Fleming's gang in the middle of it all. He knew instantly who'd been responsible for the lighthouse attacks — it was just Toff's style to give a ship-wreck a helping hand.

'You heathen thug, Fleming!' Will yelled above the roar of the waves. 'You caused this.'

Toff turned to face Will, a leer across his lips while brandishing his cudgel.

'Well, ain't yer quick enough to race down here for your share,' Toff sneered.

'Damn you, Toff. Lives will be lost tonight.'

Toff merely shrugged and turned to retrieve a cask that had just washed ashore. The wrecker's indifference so infuriated Will, he lunged forward and tackled Toff to the beach. It was a signal for a brawl to break out between the two gangs. Will and Toff rolled over the shingle thumping, kicking and clawing each another until they splashed into the sea.

Will struggled to his knees as the pebbles sucked beneath him with every wave. As he tried to stagger to his feet, they sank further. Every step was like wading in quicksand. Will's saturated coat and breeches didn't help and just as he seemed to be swept away a wave knocked him forward enabling him to scramble up the shingle to dry land. He cast his eyes around, but there was no sign of Toff Fleming.

Well, no loss, but we have other fish to fry.

'Come on, my likely lads, with me,' Will called to his men who extricated themselves from the fight. 'There is little enough we can do here. We are needed elsewhere.'

Will may have been wet and cold, but he soon warmed up as his raced towards Weymouth.

The landers left just in time, because moments later Sheriff Lightfoot and his riding officers reached Chesil beach.

What Will didn't know was Lightfoot and his men patrolled the cliff-tops that night and galloped to investigate as soon as they saw the lighthouse beacons wink out. They reached the lower light first and, just as Will had done, quickly freeing the keeper and his family. It didn't take long for Lightfoot to put two-and-two together. So leaving the keeper to restore his beacon, Lightfoot led his four men at a brisk canter towards Chesil Beach.

The riding officers lit their own torches and led their horses cautiously along the path to the beach. The sight of lawmen was enough for Toff's louts to scatter and bolt into the night. Lightfoot was just in time to see Will's gang disappear towards town, so the sheriff decided to follow that group rather than chase down individuals from Toff's gang.

Lightfoot left one of his riding officers to control the beach, ensuring any salvaged cargo was collected in the name of the crown. The scavengers from town immediately lost interest. What was the point of risking life and limb just to have your prizes confiscated?

*

Back in town Will's henchman, Stephen had raised the alarm and soon after midnight every available fishing smack and cutter made sail or rowed to sea to the rescue and possibly to pick up some valuable flotsam in the process.

Meanwhile *Sea-Snake's* crew did the same. Dandy-Jim lowered the brig's two pinnaces and the crews made several sweeps collecting a few pieces of loot as well as saving a dozen men, women and children who clung to floating wreckage.

But it didn't take long for non-swimmers to drown or succumb to hypothermia in the English Channel's chilly water. As soon as Dandy-Jim realised there was no one else to save, he recalled the pinnaces, hoisted them aboard and made way to his rendezvous with the landers.

It was dawn when *Sea-Snake* anchored just off Osmington Mills. To Dandy-Jim's relief the landers stood waiting with their carts. Stephen had joined them in Weymouth and Will's team made good time indeed. Dandy-Jim ordered the pinnaces to sea once more and his crewmen helped the shocked, cold and distraught *Lady Annabelle* survivors into the small craft. They rowed ashore with little difficulty as the reefs protected the beach by reducing the shore-break.

'Well met, Will,' Dandy-Jim greeted as he splashed ashore and the two men shook hands.

'Not quite what we planned, Jim,' Will replied. 'What have we here?'

'Survivors from the wreck — all we could find. It's been quite a night.'

'Fine. I'll have Stephen guide them to the vicarage at the Mill where Parson Phillips and his goodwife will care for them.'

Stephen left with instructions to return with all haste as there was work to do which would have been better completed by moonlight. Will estimated they had a couple of hours which should do. There was no time for Will or Dandy-Jim to ponder on the night's events or what had become of Toff Fleming.

By now *Sea-Snake's* crew had devised a speedy and efficient method of off-loading cargo. The liquor casks were roped together with glass floats tied securely at intervals along the cord although the barrels were just buoyant in salt water. In this way the casks could be hauled ashore, leaving the pinnaces to tender non water-resistant articles to the beach.

What cargo could not be loaded into Will's carts was hidden in woodland nearby. It was but fully light when Will handed a purse of guineas to Dandy-Jim. Despite Will's scuffle with Toff Fleming, the cash survived safely in the buttoned pocket of his waistcoat. The venturers would have been ill-pleased had he lost Dandy-Jim's fee.

The two men shook hands before Jim boarded the last pinnace to row back to his ship. Stephen had long returned from Osmington Mill, warning that the arrival of a dozen castaways was going to cause public interest, but no one had yet shown up at Ringstead Bay…or at least no one was seen…

*

Sheriff Lightfoot could not identify the men racing towards Weymouth, but being a suspicious man, sensed they were up to no good and had a shrewd idea what that 'no good' might be. Anyone wandering the coast by night had criminal intent in Lightfoot's eyes.

Tailing Will's band of miscreants wasn't particularly difficult. The landers made good time considering they were limited to the speed of horse traps along the path by moonlight often shadowed by tall trees along the way. Lightfoot's main problem was staying far enough behind just out of earshot, but close enough not to lose the suspected smugglers.

Lightfoot held his officers back when he saw Will gather his team on the shore of Ringstead Bay.

'Take cover in the woods,' he ordered and there they waited until *Sea-Snake* anchored.

'Now we have the scoundrels,' he hissed through his teeth as the smugglers' pinnaces rowed ashore, although he was surprised when he saw the *Lady Annabelle* survivors guided along the path to Osmington Mill Manse.

Once the path was clear he sent a man into Weymouth to alert the Weymouth Water Guard who manned a cutter especially to intercept smugglers' vessels at sea. *Lady Annabelle* had distracted the Water Guard and their cutter was at sea helping with the rescue.

His Majesty's Water Guard was a brand new service to complement the riding officers. The Weymouth detachment consisted of raw recruits and inexperienced officers. It would take time for them to return to harbour before chasing after smugglers.

Right, that takes care of things at sea, Lightfoot thought. *Now we wait.*

Lightfoot's messenger returned in an hour. Although outnumbered two-to-one, the riding officers pounced as soon as all the contraband was ashore and Dandy-Jim had returned to his vessel.

'Stand fast you rascals,' Sheriff Lightfoot growled. 'My armed agents will take down the first man who moves.'

At daybreak and with the help of torchlight, the riding officers now had light enough to see their targets. And they weren't armed with inaccurate Brown Bess muskets, but with modern, rifled carbines and a brace of loaded pistols tucked into each of their belts. The landers were caught red-handed.

Dandy-Jim on the other hand was long gone before the Water Guard cutter gave chase. *Sea-Snake* vanished over the horizon aided by a brisk following wind which sprang up by mid-morning.

Leaving a man to guard the contraband, Sheriff Lightfoot's riding officers escorted Will and his comrades to the Weymouth watch-house and saw them safely deposited behind bars.

Now that might not have been as bad as it looked. Often local magistrates were also venturers and usually let the offenders off with a light fine before confiscating the contraband for redistribution much as it was originally intended. Fines were more likely than not subsidised by other venturers and the community at large. Smuggling was good for the local economy, and no one wanted to stop the supply of consumables.

Sheriff Lightfoot might have been a joyless prig, but he was conscientious and he certainly wasn't a fool. His first action was to send word to the chief constable stationed at Dorchester, who quickly summoned the principal district judge to preside over the case — and His Honour, Judge Lord John Ball was a stern fellow not well disposed towards smugglers, or criminals of any form, for that matter.

Two highwaymen and a deranged woman who'd stabbed her abusive husband to death still dangled from a gibbet outside Dorchester Old Court and Cells complex as an example to future miscreants. A week later Judge Ball refused to have the corpses removed even when the mayor protested they'd turned putrid and the contents of their bowels lay splattered on the cobblestones below.

That was the virtuous stalwart Will and his men faced when they were charged a few hours later. The waters were muddied further by *Lady Annabelle* foundering right in the middle of the night's adventure. The wreck broke up during the next day, but thanks to Will and Stephen's quick action many lives were saved. *Lady Annabelle's* master had wisely decided to go down with his ship, because he was in deep trouble with the Company's board of inquiry. But the heavy hand of the law was unlikely to show mercy…

Chapter 3 — The Deal

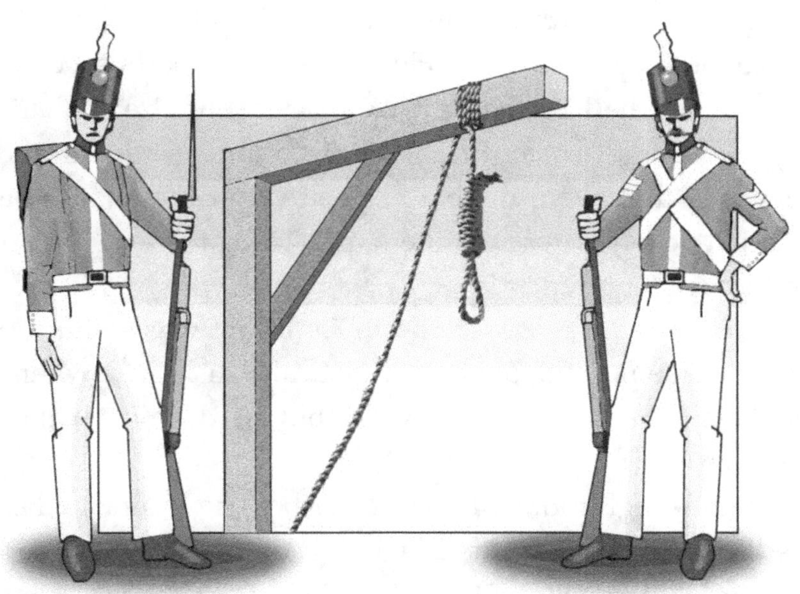

There was no time for the landers to appoint a defence lawyer — even if they could afford one. Sheriff Lightfoot and Judge Ball wanted the matter dealt with in haste.

'The crown will prove these men, with scant regard for human life, did wantonly extinguish the Portland Bill higher and lower lights,' urbane prosecutor, Sir David Warren announced in his opening address, 'thus causing the East Indiaman, *Lady Annabelle,* to lose its way and dash to pieces off shore with great loss of life.'

Although the investigation hadn't even opened at the time, ultimately it determined only twelve people perished in the wreck, which wasn't perhaps 'great loss of life', but tragic enough if you happened to be one of the dead dozen. From the outset the trial went south for Will, Stephen and their fellow landers. Worst of all they were charged with extinguishing the Portland Bill lights.

The problem was Toff Fleming's body hadn't been found while his gang had bolted and were probably already out of the county. Sir David so confused the lighthouse keepers and their families that they were unable to positively differentiate between who had attacked or rescued them and Toff's mates were nowhere around to be identified.

To make matters worse Sheriff Lightfoot was so hungry for a result he did something uncharacteristically dishonest when giving his evidence. He didn't actually lie, but he didn't tell the whole truth either.

'Sheriff Lightfoot, please describe the scene when you reached Chesil Beach after delivering the lighthouse keepers to safety,' Sir David began with an infuriating suave voice, giving the impression he was totally indifferent to the proceedings and above the riff-raff with whom he was forced to share the court room.

'There were lots of folk on the beach, sir — waiting for anything that washed up from the wreck.'

'Was there much wreckage?'

'A fair bit, sir, but some had already been spirited away. The crowd dispersed when we arrived and initially I posted men to gather and guard any cargo that landed.'

'Did you try to round up the crowd?'

'I did not have sufficient men to do so, sir.'

'But you arrested the defendants?'

'Yes, I saw a group leaving Chesil for Weymouth. I then left one man on Chesil Beach and ordered my remaining fellows to follow them, sir. I considered the best use of my resources.'

'Most commendable, I'm sure.'

Lightfoot went on to describe the arrest accurately enough, but failed to mention Toff Fleming or his gang, simply saying Will's men were smugglers caught in the act. Presumably Lightfoot didn't want talk of Toff Fleming et al as they were well known villains who'd got clean away — a fact that might jeopardise a conviction. Ultimately he needn't have worried Lord Ball was going to ensure justice was *seen* to be done. Once the prosecution was complete he turned to the dock and glared at the accused.

'What do you have to say for yourselves?' His Lordship demanded.

'We never put the lights out, milord,' Will protested. 'We were the coves who untied the higher light keeper.'

'He did not appear to be totally convinced of that fact,' Lord Ball challenged.

'He'd been coshed, milord and bleary-eyed and his kin were scare half out of their wits.'

'Indeed it hardly makes them reliable witnesses either, does it now?'

'Well no, milord.'

'And that, sir is unfortunate for you and your cohorts.'

'You have to believe me, milord!'

'In which case, what business took you so coincidentally to the cliff-tops, may I ask?'

And there lay the rub. Will's business was smuggling and he had no excuse other than he was there to meet *Sea-Snake*, so why would he want the lighthouses out of commission? The smugglers' vessel needed the beacons for guidance just as much as *Lady Annabelle's* crew. Only Dandy-Jim's peerless seamanship, local knowledge and the upcoming moon had saved another wreck. But to say as much was admitting to being a smuggler, which was also a charge serious enough to merit the gibbet in Lord Ball's view. He wasn't a venturer so disinclined to leniency.

Will tried to convince the Lord Ball he and his men had simply heard about *Lady Annabelle* and joined the crowd. Unfortunately the judge didn't believe him and the rest was a mere formality.

The loss of human life was the deciding factor for Lord Ball. To horrified gasps from the public gallery, the judge donned his black cap and promptly condemned Will to the gallows — may God have mercy on his soul. Will's gang members were each sentenced to seven years penal servitude in the New South Wales Colony.

It was an era of swift justice. Will's comrades were whisked away in chains and transported by prison carriage fifty miles to Portsmouth. There they were incarcerated below decks aboard former French prize, *HMS Prothée*, a sixty-four gun third-rater now reduced to a prison hulk. There in the fetid stench they awaited a ship to carry them to Sydney Town.

Meanwhile Will remained in the Dorchester lockup.

Christina was of course devastated and had rushed to Dorchester with her parents for the trial. They stayed at *The Ship Inn* so Christina could visit the Old Crown Court and Cells every day. The good Reverend Proud petitioned the court on Will's behalf, but his entreaties were steadfastly rejected by Judge Ball. Indeed it appeared only intervention from the Privy Council could save Will, and that might take months — even years.

And time wasn't something Will had on his side. His execution was scheduled for the following week. Christina's desolation and sense of loss were profound. She was a passionate girl who enjoyed the intimacy and companionship of married life. Despite his occasional nightly rendezvous with *Sea-Snake,* Will was an attentive and cheerful husband whom she loved in her honest well-meaning way.

Now he was to be cruelly snatched away after they'd been wed only a few weeks…

*

2nd Infantry Battalion, 1st Dorset Yeomanry Regiment Barracks, Yeovil

Lieutenant Colonel Sir Rodney Weaver and his 2IC Major Henry Jameison were in a bind. They were under orders to join Lord Wellesley's force in Portugal, but the battalion was just over half strength — barely five companies.

'Dammit, Jameison,' the colonel protested, 'we're in danger of being dispersed into other units before we even go abroad. We must make a better showing than this.'

'Yes, sir,' Jameson replied calmly. 'Our subalterns have sections scouring every corner of the county right at this very moment.'

*

Christina brought Will treats every day, although in truth he had little appetite. A week to the gibbet can have that effect on a man. The constable in charge of the Old Court Cells didn't object to Christina entering Will's cell and became downright co-operative when she allowed him to pilfer tit-bits after he'd searched her picnic hamper.

Christina was market shopping when a platoon of redcoats marched along High West Street. She turned to see a striking young officer mounted on a fine grey mare lead the column while a tough, scar-faced sergeant brought up the rear to ensure there were no stragglers.

The young officer halted his column and dismounted right in front of the Old Court Cells. The single epaulette on his right shoulder marked him as a lieutenant.

'Split the men into sections, Sergeant Newell,' he said wearily. 'All the usual places, if you please — the men know the drill by now. Come with me and we'll see what the gaol-house has to offer.'

'You 'eard Mister McAlister, lads,' Jack Newell barked. ''Op to it, lively now.'

The redcoats clattered off in all directions. Lieutenant McAlister didn't look at all dismayed when one section of men entered the nearest inn, while others hurried on to different drinking establishments.

'Very well, Sergeant Newell, let's see what the local peace-keepers have for us.'

Normally Lieutenant McAlister would have dealt with Lord Ball, but his lordship had returned to his estate leaving Sheriff Lightfoot in charge of the courthouse and gaol. Whereas Ball was looking forward to a decent hanging, Lightfoot had misgivings. Will had always protested his innocence and Lightfoot was coming to think he'd been over-hasty and should have investigated Toff Fleming's role in the *Lady Annabelle* wreck more thoroughly.

But McAlister had an offer that might appease the sheriff's conscience. The lieutenant handed Lightfoot the South Britain

Division recruiting warrant authorizing him to offer prisoners a pardon in exchange for seven year's military service.

'You'll have to go to the Portsmouth hulks, sir,' Lightfoot explained. 'I only have one man here and he is condemned to hang in a few days.'

'Then I daresay my proposition will be of profound interest to him,' McAlister observed blandly.

'I believe it is a matter for Lord Ball…' Lightfoot began.

'Nonsense, man,' McAlister retorted with commendable authority for such a young fellow. 'His Majesty needs every man we can muster. I believe the South Britain Division wishes will be sufficient for his lordship — who does appear to be absent. That leaves you in charge, Sheriff Lightfoot. I am sure you have no desire to disappoint His Majesty and hinder Britain's war effort against the tyrant Bonaparte.'

Lightfoot was out of his depth.

'Very well, sir,' the sheriff conceded. 'If you will follow me, you may put your proposal to the prisoner.'

*

Christina arrived at the Courthouse steps just as Will was being escorted from the building.

'What is the meaning of this, sir?' she challenged the young lieutenant.

'Stand aside, miss,' Sergeant Newell growled. 'This man 'as just enlisted. It's a fine life of adventure for 'im now, so it is.'

Christina was dumbfounded. Her basket fell to the ground.

'What…? He is my…husband…'

'Begging your pardon, madam,' McAlister said, touching his shako peak. 'I suggest the alternative was hardly more appealing.'

'Sorry, love,' Will shrugged. 'It was sign up or the rope.'

'Silence!' Newell snapped

'But you shall be gone forever,' Christina wailed.

'Seven years actually,' McAlister corrected.

'It might as well be forever. How can I live knowing you're hundreds of miles away? You cannot leave me. I will not permit it.'

'You ain't in no position…' Sergeant Newell snapped.

'Now steady on, Newell, can you not see Mrs Jenkins is distressed?'

'Aye, sir, but that ain't our business.'

'Possibly not, but as this couple was married before Jenkins enlisted, his wife is entitled to be included on company strength with half-rations. I cannot see Colonel Weaver objecting, can you, Sergeant?'

'Ain't for me to say what colonels object to, sir,' Newell shrugged. He was indifferent and this little filly was so young and easy on the eye.

'I do not understand what you are saying, sir,' Christina stared wide-eyed.

'Then I shall enlighten you, madam,' McAlister said. 'King's regulations permit recruits' wives to live with them in barracks. If you wish to accompany your husband, I suggest you report to the Dorset Yeomanry Barracks as soon as possible. But I admonish you madam, there is nothing dainty about barracks life.'

'Do not worry about that, sir. I shall be there first thing tomorrow.'

And so despite Reverend and Mrs Proud's vehement protests, Christina came to follow the drum.

2nd Infantry Battalion, 1st Dorset Yeomanry Regiment Barracks, Yeovil

Christina had no knowledge of barracks life and she was in for a shock. Battalion quarters were noisy, profane and overcrowded. Slatted bed and bunks line the sides of long dormitories housing up to fifty soldiers and in some cases their wives. Blankets made make-shift screens, but privacy and personal space were virtually non-existent especially if you felt frisky…*and* Christina and Will were a boisterous couple.

While the soldiers drilled endlessly, their women toiled in a steaming laundry or occupied themselves repairing uniforms. It was hard work with long hours, but Christina was pleased to receive some extra cash from single men who had little time for their own washing. The women also ensured the latrines and wash-houses were hygienically acceptable, which although a thoroughly unpleasant task was better than allowing human waste to become overpowering.

Christina quickly understood just how squalid military life could be.

Two elements of barracks life especially distressed Christina who'd being brought up in a God-fearing manner. Coarse language caused her to blush initially, but she was a pragmatic girl and soon got used to the blasphemy and expletives. She also learned that some wives prostituted themselves and boasted how lucrative that could be.

'Do not expect me to become a whore,' she admonished Will one night as they turned in for the night.

'Goodness me, my love, the thought had never crossed my mind,' he grinned. 'But now that you mention it...'

She punched him and snuffed out the candle. They made love to the snores and flatulence of sleeping men. That intimacy helped Christina shut out her environment for a short while. Much as she regretted their new life, she never once considered abandoning Will and returning to Cerne Abbas. Christina was naturally charitable, industrious, adaptable and most of all — loyal.

The military wives were a raucous bunch, but generally good natured although there were occasional bullies who tried to throw their weight around. Christina soon abandoned any genteel ways and learnt to stand her ground. She discovered that any woman trying to push her around backed down when challenged.

Although Will said Lieutenant McAlister was much involved in the men's training, Christina saw nothing of the handsome young officer. Sergeant Newell inspected the barracks occasionally. He didn't appear too particular about the men's living conditions, but eyed their women-folk lasciviously. Christina disliked the sergeant instantly and steered clear whenever he was close by.

Newell's voice boomed continuously from the parade ground as he drilled the men endlessly. Often by nightfall, Will would return to the barracks barely able to stand after enduring Newell's extra punishment drill for any tiny infringement. On many occasions the company marched to a nearby cow paddock to conduct live musketry training.

Will was a born marksman and experienced rabbit hunter with a fowling piece, but that was not essential during volley fire from the weighty ten-and-a-half pound Brown Bess flintlock muskets. The gunnery instructors were more interested in rate-of-fire rather than accuracy, simply instructing the recruits to aim low as the musket kicked like a mule, jerking the barrel upwards. The weapon's effective range was no more than a hundred yards and probably only half that in the heat of battle. Not that anyone could tell as they were enveloped in clouds of gun smoke with every shot and judging what you'd hit was problematic.

One evening Will returned from duty with news.

'We are to be posted to Portugal to join General Wellesley's army,' he announced. 'We sail from Portsmouth next week. Mister McAlister is well pleased because we can now fire four rounds a minute. That as good as any regiment in 'is lordship's army.'

Everyone knew this was coming, but it was especially heart-breaking for the soldiers' wives. Only six wives per company were permitted to accompany the battalion overseas while the remainder were abandoned and no longer qualified to draw military entitlements. Some could return home or rely on parish charity, but others were simply destined for a life on the streets or the workhouse.

The accepted practice was for six lucky — or unlucky — females to be selected by ballot...

Chapter 4 — Portugal

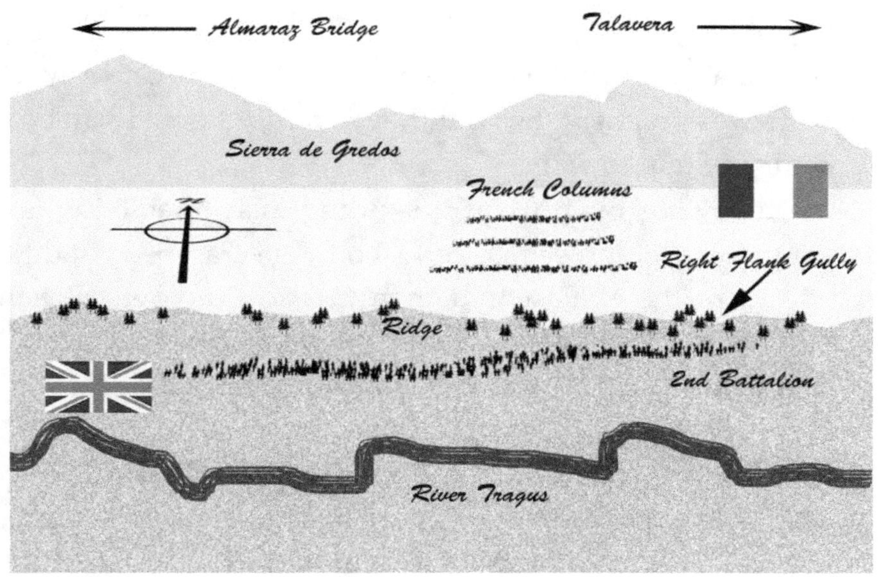

Christina may have been sanguine, but Will was appalled when she was selected as one of the half-dozen wives to accompany the battalion.

'You will be safer if you return to you parents,' Will said. 'I will come for you when I am able.'

'What — in seven years..?'

'We may not be gone that long. I mean how long does it take to beat a bunch of poxy frog-eaters?'

'Quite some time, by all accounts. It seems this war has gone on forever. I will not wait forever, Will.'

'You would find another?'

'Do not be silly. Of course I would not countenance such a thing. I am your wife and your wife I shall remain. I promised to stay beside you through thick and thin and that is precisely what I intend to do.'

Christina also withheld a secret from Will because had he known she was pregnant, he would have refused point blank to let her accompany him to war.

The following month was a swirling mist of activity as the battalion mobilized and sailed for Lisbon. The cramped conditions below decks of the ex-East Indiaman *Cecilia Bond* were abysmal. Each soldier was assigned a hammock which brushed against his neighbour's, but scant provision had been made for baggage — or wives.

But Christina was content to sleep below Will's hammock on a bed made of his pack and their spare clothing. She was normally so exhausted, she had little trouble sleeping. Although she didn't suffer, Christina spent most of the two week voyage nursing sea-sickness victims. She cherished the brief occasions she was permitted to walk on the main-deck and savour pristine sea air. The ocean's vastness and power were awesome and Christina delighted at the wonder of dolphins darting through *Cecilia Bond's* bow-wave.

The mighty Royal Navy flotilla was just as majestic. Since Trafalgar four years earlier, Britannia truly ruled the waves, reducing the French to a purely land force. Indeed British warships blockaded all major continental ports. Only sleek, maneuverable vessels crewed by daring experts such as Dandy-Jim Mullins slipped through the screen of man-o-wars. The risks were enormous, but so was the profit.

In time the fleet reached Lisbon and unloaded the 2nd Battalion, men, weapons, officers' mounts and portmanteaux, baggage, camp-followers and all. Two days later they were ready march inland and reinforce the Wellesley's force at a place smack in the middle of Spain called Talavera. As Wellesley's force had done, the battalion followed the route along the Tragus River Valley, but was often diverted through narrow paths barely wide enough for infantry let alone their baggage and ammunition wagons.

Even covering thirty miles a day, Colonel Sir Rodney Weaver fretted that his battalion was travelling too slowly and would miss the upcoming battle. Wellesley was spoiling for a fight while Marshal Claude Victor and General Horace Sebastiani were ready to oblige him.

Dear God, how can anyone endure this heat? Christina wondered, yearning for a mild English summer afternoon under a giant oak or elm. She trudged with a party of women behind the main body of troops who travelled in companies divided into platoons so officers and NCOs were spread along the column to ensure there were no stragglers.

Fortunately they often travelled close to the river and gratefully bathed at every bivouac. Modesty was not an option and Christina soon learnt to ignore the whistles and ribald cat-calls from the ranks as she bathed bare-breasted with the other women.

Christina recorded her daily routine in a neatly written journal, which mostly described the tedium, heat and fatigue, but maintained an underlining optimism and cheerfulness despite the continuing drudgery.

There was a singular entry dated in late July…

Lieutenant McAlister was fastidious about his men's health, insisting his men bathe regularly. He inspected their feet for signs of blisters and fungal outbreaks.

'You pamper them, Mr. McAlister,' Sergeant Newell protested mildly. 'You ain't their mamma, sir.'

'We are infantry, Sergeant,' Jonathan replied evenly, 'our feet are as important as our muskets.'

Cleanliness and dryness appeared to be the best and easiest solutions, so Christina ensured Will's feet were in perfect marching condition. Nor did she neglect her own, knowing she must keep up with the column or be left behind.

They trudged on to Talavera where Colonel Weaver's worst fears were realised. Wellesley's force was nowhere to be seen!

But there was no mistaking where they'd been.

Christina was horrified to see the ground littered with hundreds of corpses already attracting blizzards of flies, crows, buzzards, rats and other carrion-feeding opportunists. Some men lay in ragged uniforms but many had been stripped by scavengers, who'd carried away anything valuable during the night. There were reports that wounded men were clubbed to death if they resisted the nighthawks.

Red-hot cannon balls and exploding shells had gouged great swathes of land, igniting the tinder-dry grass land. Charred bodies lay where they had fallen. Those who'd died instantly were spared the torment of others too badly wounded to escape the flames.

Sir Rodney ordered his men to halt on high ground overlooking Talavera. Although he didn't know it his battalion now occupied the British and Spanish positions during the battle south of Portina Creek, a tributary of River Tagus.

'Major Jameison, I would be much obliged if you will lead a company into town and discover the situation within those walls, sir.'

'Aye, Sir Rodney. It all seems too quiet for my liking. Towns should be rowdy, bustling places,' Jameison replied cautiously.

'There has been a stiff fight here recently. No doubt that would dampen any jollity.'

But Jameison wasn't needed in the end. As the senior officers spoke two riders passed through a city gate and rode casually towards the battalion ranks. One of the riders was unremarkable, dressed in smart but well-worn civilian clothes. A sensible broad-brimmed hat protected him from the sun. The other horseman was unmistakable as a British redcoat major. Resplendent in his uniform and shako, he was so strikingly handsome Christina found it hard not to stare.

The arrivals rode past Will's company, but halted close enough to be within earshot.

The uniformed officer saluted crisply while his companion doffed his hat.

'Good day to you, Sir Rodney,' the civilian greeted. 'I fear the battle is done…'

'As I see, sir,' Sir Rodney replied curtly. He didn't need anyone reminding him he'd missed the action. 'You seem well informed, but I regret you have the advantage over me.'

'Information is our business, we are General Wellesley's exploring officers,' the major smiled. 'I am Major Colquhoun Grant — 11th Foot regiment — and permit me to present my colleague, Lieutenant Colonel Sir John Waters of 1st Royal Scots Foot, now seconded to the Portuguese Army.'

'Honoured I am sure, gentlemen,' Sir Rodney said, 'but am I to understand you are spies?'

'Indeed, sir,' Waters chuckled, 'we are in the intelligence business, but the title doesn't sit as well with some as it does with others, eh Grant?'

'I prefer my uniform thank you, Sir John,' Grant replied. 'I consider myself a scout and as you well know the Froggies will shoot you if they catch you in mufti.'

'I am hard to spot, sir.'

'Gentlemen…' Sir Rodney insisted. 'The situation, if you would be so kind…and where the blue blazes is General Wellesley?'

'Oh, the army is long gone,' Grant said airily. 'Do you not realise Marshall Soult is advancing from the north with thirty thousand men?'

'I was indeed unaware of that particular fact, sir.'

'You might consider employing your own exploring officers, colonel.'

Sir Rodney was *considering* admonishing Grant for impertinence, but let it slide as the exploring officers explained the previous weeks' events. Talavera had been fought to a stalemate although the British claimed victory because the French withdrew first. Napoleon's older brother Joseph — the nominal French commander — and Marshall Jourdan — the actual French commander, had lost enthusiasm for the fight after heavy losses. They failed to press several advantages and finally retreated towards Madrid.

Wellesley initially planned to give chase, but changed his mind once he heard the news that Marshall Soult was on his way to join the fight. General Robert Craufurd's light infantry brigade reinforced Wellesley's army, but had arrived too late to help despite marching forty odd miles in twenty-four hours to the battlefield. In any event a single brigade was not enough.

'General Wellesley deemed it prudent to withdraw ahead of Marshall Soult's advance,' Sir John explained. 'He was forced to leave fifteen hundred wounded in town and he has abandoned our Spanish allies to their own devices.'

'Craufurd's men have dashed back to hold the bridge across the Tagus River Tagus at Almaraz, so the army can regroup to the west.'

'Dear God this is preposterous,' Sir Rodney spluttered. 'We followed that confounded river all the way here. How is it we did not meet the returning army?'

Sir Rodney's tactful use of *returning* rather than *retreating* was not lost on Lieutenant Jonathan McAlister over-hearing the senior officers.

'There is a road, you know,' Grant replied blandly. 'It's a bit of a track really that runs north of the river. I'm surprised Wellesley's scouts did not cross your path, but I do believe the general was more concerned about his northern flank.'

'I would advise you to do the same, colonel,' Waters added. 'And I would not be inclined to dawdle.'

'But, what is to become the wounded men?' Major Jameison interjected.

'The Spanish will move as many as possible as far from the enemy as they can manage, but I fear those remaining will become prisoners. They are in greater peril from Spanish looters and guerrillas than the French anyway.'

There was nothing else to do but bivouac for the night and follow Wellesley's column back to Portugal. After giving orders for his men to salvage all the weapons, munitions and stores they could scrounge, Sir Rodney and Major Jamieson visited Talavera. The two senior officers returned dispirited because they couldn't help the wounded soldiers who would remained billeted in town until the French arrived and took them prisoner.

With four extra cartloads of weaponry, the battalion was on the march before dawn. Mules to haul the carts had been problematic until Sergeant Newell led a squad into town and commandeered a beast for each cart.

Grant joined the battalion, while Waters' duties took him elsewhere. They marched along the track running parallel to the river and it wasn't a hard trail to follow. The British army had abandoned any unnecessary baggage, littering the countryside as it went. Christina was surprised at the number of duchesses lying by the roadside. British officers apparently loathed to travel light until push came to shove, forcing them to get a move on.

And it wasn't long before the French turned up. Not a vast horde to be sure, but a troop of lancers on patrol and looking for mischief. About twenty-five horsemen rode along a low ridge only a few hundred yards from the battalion right flank. Occasionally a spy-glass glinted in the sun as the patrol assessed Sir Rodney's force.

'I do not care for those rascals staring down at us, Jamieson,' Sir Rodney declared peevishly. 'Please oblige me by sending half a company of our stout fellows to see them off.'

Jamieson ordered platoons one, two and three from A Company to form in three ranks and advance towards the lancers. McAlister led his men of the third platoon, while Colquhoun Grant came along to identify the Frenchmen. He felt there was nothing to fear, because despite their wicked lances, a handful of horsemen was unlikely to cause a tight infantry formation much trouble.

Indeed that proved to be correct. The French cavalry withdrew almost languidly, disappearing below the ridgeline. As Jamieson's men reached the crest, the major ordered a halt. A plain stretched beyond the ridge towards undulating country before rearing into the Sierra de Gredos range.

A body of troops was just visible in the distance.

'Half brigade strength I believe,' Jamieson assayed.

'Correct, sir,' Grant confirmed. 'Colonel Henri L'Strande's demi-brigade if I am not mistaken.'

'You know of this unit?' Jamieson queried.

'Indeed, sir. They're recently conscripted troops bound to join Soult no doubt. See they have but a company of voltigeurs-of-the-line and no grenadiers whatsoever. They are untried infantry, sir.'

'As are we,' Jamieson observed guardedly.

'My compliments to Sir Rodney and ask him he would kindly join us if you please, McAlister,' the major added with commendable composure.

Just as the colonel came up the ridge the French lancers reached their brigade and within moments the entire force veered left and headed straight towards the Dorset battalion.

'They intend to fight us,' Sir Rodney declared.

'I believe that to be so, colonel,' Grant agreed.

It soon became apparent that the French outnumbered 2nd Battalion two-to-one, but the Dorset men held the high ground and it would be the devil's work for the French to storm up the rocky defile with British muskets pouring lead into them. Furthermore there was a degree of tree cover along the ridge, but the naked plain afforded L'Strande's force no protection at all.

'I will not have my brave fellows cowering behind trees,' Sir Rodney admonished. 'We will face the froggies with pride.'

'I daresay,' Grant ventured, 'but there is no point in exposing your men needlessly. You will need them all. See these rock formations will serve you well and you'll still have a clear firing line.'

'Perhaps you are right. We will use what God has provided. Bring our men up from the river, if you please Jamieson,' Sir

Rodney said. 'Deploy them along the ridge. Bring up all the ammunition wagons. You know what to do.'

'And the camp followers, sir?'

'They will stay where they are. Safest place for 'em I believe.'

Jamieson dispatched Jonathan McAlister with the orders adding it would be a good idea to be nippy about it.

Soon men were scrambling up from the river and forming inline along the ridge. The ammunition carts were heavy and proved difficult to bring into position until Christina, the lottery wives and a dozen other women who'd joined the column lent a hand and pushed for all they were worth.

By the time 2nd Battalion had formed up it was late afternoon and the French were at the foot of the ridge. A brace of cannons stood behind the infantry. Suddenly two gouts of smoke belched from the barrels followed by the crump of an explosion a second later. Every one heard the ball whistle overhead only to bounce harmlessly down the ridge, landing with a splash in the river.

Wellesley's army had superbly trained artillerymen and well maintained cannons, but they were scarce and 2nd Battalion had no heavy fire support.

The second French salvo smashed into the ridge in front of the British line, spraying rock and scree spectacularly, but doing no damage other than spooking the officers' mounts. Either the French gunners were inexperienced or short of ammunition, because the rate of artillery fire was sporadic and inaccurate. It would be up to infantry to finish the job.

Sir Rodney saw little threat to his front. The French would first have to scramble uphill under withering fire, which was a task even seasoned troops would baulk at. But both British flanks were at risk especially the right which ended by a gully where the

French could channel their fusiliers with less difficulty. This is where they'd most likely advance and it was not lost on the battalion commander.

Chapter 5 — First Blood

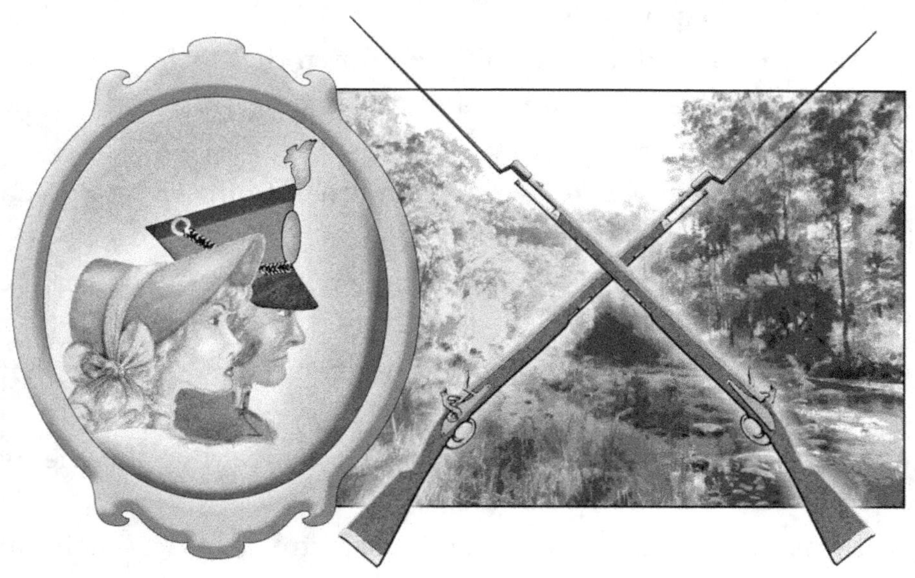

'You will send a company of our best fellows to the right, Jamieson,' Sir Rodney declared. 'I will not have those villains troubling our flank. I simply will not have it.'

Major Jamieson led 'A' company to the right with McAlister's platoon in the van. They reached the gully in a moment and saw the danger. The path was indeed narrow where men could only advance three abreast, but it was clear the track was well used by locals. The French infantry would have no difficulty climbing to the ridgeline.

'We will form our line here,' Jamieson surmised. 'We'll pour lead into the froggies when they try to squeeze through this gap.'

'Sir, I may see an opportunity,' Jonathan ventured.

'Please explain, McAlister and do be brief. I believe our enemy is about to enter that pathway.'

Jonathan outlined his plan in seconds. Jamieson nodded.

'You'll need to be damned quick. We'll hold the line here and make it hot for those rascals.'

Jonathan saluted and led his men down the track. What had caught his eye were the boulders and tree line on either side of the track.

'Sergeant Newell, take every second man to the right. Spread out behind cover and await my command.'

'Yessir,' Newell acknowledged and led half the platoon to the right.

Meanwhile Jonathan urged his remaining men to the left where the cover was less, but would have to do. They were just in time because soon they heard drummer-boys heralding the enemy advance.

It was impossible to gauge the French strength as the column stretched beyond sight. The fusiliers grimly marched forward with disciplined determination. All wore moustaches in the French infantry tradition. Their uniforms bore green and yellow trim identifying the men as fusiliers. They held their muskets at the ready with bayonets attached.

With their focus on the path ahead, the French failed to notice the redcoats, crouching only metres away on either side. Jonathan knew his luck wouldn't last. The longer he waited, the greater chance of detection, but he wanted at least half a company to pass and face Major Jamieson's muskets.

As it turned out the several Frenchmen spotted Jonathan's men. They stared open-mouthed as he gave the order.

'Volley fire…fire!'

Thirty barrels erupted, blazing lead into French column at lethally close range.

'Reload! Fire at will!'

'Mark your target. Make every shot count,' Sergeant Newell ordered. 'This ain't volley fire now. Kill the bastards!'

The gully was immediately shrouded in smoke, confusing the French while giving the redcoats time to reload. Jonathan heard the rattle of muskets as the leading Frenchmen marched into Jamieson's first volley.

The French casualties were horrific. About twenty men lay dead and as many wounded writhed among the rocks. The second round of sporadic musketry was less devastating, but drove the French back in a rush, smashing into those coming from behind in confusion which led to panic…and panic is infectious.

In no time the French were in full retreat without really knowing why.

Will Jenkins stood beside Jonathan and gave a whoop as he knew both his shots had hit their mark.

'Fine work, lads,' Jonathan said, 'but they'll be back. Reload and fix bayonets.'

Meanwhile Newell had ordered his men to do the same. Once the smoke settled, the sergeant ordered his men to break cover and finish off the French wounded with cold steel.

Initially Jonathan wasn't sure what they were up to, but was appalled when he saw the butchery even though he knew they had come to kill the French and that was precisely what Newell was doing ruthlessly.

'Get your men back in position, Sergeant,' Jonathan yelled. 'I don't want them caught in the open when the French return.'

And return they did…and they were more cautious the second time around.

This time they sent skirmishers who used the cover to advance and start peppering away with accurate musket-fire.

Meanwhile the fusiliers regrouped, massing at the foot of the ridge to advance once more.

So the fight developed into a scrappy brawl of scattered musketry and frequent individual bayonet duels. The gully was a natural funnel for gun smoke which drifted down the slope, often obliterating any sight of the combatants. This gave some bold souls the opportunity to advance and cause damage, but mostly both sides were content to remain under cover sniping away when they saw a chance.

While a stalemate developed in the gully, Sir Rodney easily contained the centre while the French gave up on the left flank as the terrain was practically impassable at the best of time let alone under a hail of lead balls.

As the day progressed redcoat casualties remained mercifully low, with only a few flesh wounds and so far all Jonathan's platoon was still in action. But their ammunition was running low. Soon the redcoat position would become untenable unless they were resupplied with cartridges and shot.

'Jenkins, get back up to Major Jamieson and tell him the tale,' Jonathan said to Will. 'We need ammunition on both sides of the track.'

Jamieson's position was about two hundred yards uphill and the path was littered with dead and grievously wounded fusiliers. The remaining company had not advanced. Jamieson obviously judged their field of fire was best where they stood. The number of French casualties appeared to validate that assessment.

So Will was flabbergasted when he met Christina and the other lottery wives half way to the British line. Each woman had two muskets slung over their shoulders, carrying cartridge and shot boxes between them.

'What are you doing?' Will said. 'You're supposed to be back at the river.'

'That seems to be the only place the Frenchie cannon balls are landing, so we thought we'd make ourselves useful,' Christina explained while her companions nodded in unison.

'Heavens woman — it's dangerous. The frogs are just down the hill.'

'I don't think anywhere is particularly safe, my dear. Now do you want this powder or not?'

'I can't believe Major Jamieson let you come down here.'

'We sort of snuck passed him,' one of the wives giggled. 'We left him spluttering and ordering us back, but I fancy we misunderstood him.'

Much as Jonathan appreciated the ammunition and extra muskets, he was speechless when the womenfolk showed up. When he finally found words, Christina had already assessed the situation, sending three women with half the boxes across to Newell. What the sergeant made of the development was unsure. He simply ordered the women to distribute the powder and shot among his men.

About then the French did what they should have done sooner. Their artillery was virtually ineffective simply blasting boulders or firing cannonballs overhead. Finally the gunners limbered up one of the heavy weapons and the horse teams moved it towards the ravine.

The path was by no means straight, but the guns tore a way through after two six-pound balls crashed into rock and forestry. Will Jenkins was only yards from cover when a third ball sprayed his upper torso to pulp before bouncing upward into Major Jamieson's line and wiping out several more infantrymen.

Fortunately Christina was distributing ammunition and was spared the spectacle of her husband's death. His corpse from the waist down now lay among the dead Frenchmen and was unidentifiable. And she was not to discover the tragedy for some time…

After softening up the British line with half-a-dozen salvoes the French infantry advanced yet again. This time they were more circumspect, using any cover available as they approached. Once the musketry resumed the cover was simply powder smoke that blocked any chance of firing at an actual target.

Jonathan's platoon was now in danger of being overrun. Although they poured musket fire in the direction of the French, they could not bring a target to bear and were firing blind. To make matters worse fusiliers would rush their position with fixed bayonets ending in hand-to-hand brawls with the redcoats.

Jonathan ordered his men to withdraw to Major Jamieson's line then darted across the gully and told Newell to do the same. Jonathan's men escaped just yards ahead of the French leaving five dead comrades including Will Jenkins. The only good thing Jonathan could report to Jamieson was the cannons had ceased firing now Frenchmen blocked the trail.

But as night fell and the light failed the fight petered out both in the gully and along the ridgeline where Sir Rodney's line hadn't wavered or suffered major casualties. Jamieson had held the flank although his butcher's bill was greatest with ten dead and several wounded.

2nd Battalion bivouacked along the ridgeline for the night. They erected crude shelters from blankets as there was no time or space to pitch tents. It was then Christina sought her husband and learnt the awful truth…and from the least sympathetic source.

Sergeant Newell grabbed her roughly pawing her breasts and buttocks.

'Take you hands off me, you brute,' Christina screamed, wrenching free and slapping his face. 'I am a married woman with child and not for you.'

'Think I don't know whelp-swell when I see it?' Newell snarled. 'But I don't pay that no mind now, 'cos you ain't a wife no more, you ain't,' Newell sneered. 'Your Will ain't no more. He's dead as a maggot — sliced in two by a cannonball.'

It took a moment for that particular piece of information to penetrate.

'I do not believe you.'

'You don't, eh? Just ask the lads then. Seems none of 'em has pumped up the courage to tell yer yet.'

Christina stared at Newell whose eyes pierced like the devil as they reflected the campfire flames. And there was worse to come.

'Now your old man's gone you ain't on battalion strength no more unless you hitch up with someone right smartish especially as you're in the family way.'

Newell added casting his eyes to Christina's belly.

'It don't mean yer honey-trap ain't still ready for use, and I've 'ad me eye on you for some time, missie. There ain't no doubt you're feisty little filly and it'll be my job to tame yer. Sergeants get first chance at widows I fancy. '

Newell lunged again, grabbing Christina by the wrist before cuffing her savagely, knocking her to her knees...

Jonathan McAlister was returning from Colonel Weaver's HQ tent with instructions for the night, ever alert for deserters and French activity. To the side he heard a woman scream. That was not unusual. The battalion was a rambunctious place and camp-followers often prone to hysterics. Nevertheless he went to investigate.

In the dimness beneath tree shadows Jonathan spotted Jack Newell towering above a cringing woman with his clenched fist raised and ready to strike. Stepping forward, Jonathan drew his pistol and gently placed the barrel against Newell's temple. The sergeant froze as he heard the pistol's hammer click into its cocked position.

'Sergeant Newell,' he whispered coolly, 'I will not tolerate the abuse of a lady from anyone in my platoon — anyone in the battalion for that matter.'

'This ain't no lady, sir,' Newell replied. 'And meanin' no disrespect, sir, soldier's affairs ain't no business for officers.'

'I daresay, Sergeant Newell, but my men's welfare is. How can they sleep with this hullabaloo? They're edgy enough as it is. We have a busy day tomorrow, do you not think?'

Newell was about to say more, but Jonathan spoke first.

'Sir Rodney has ordered us to resume our positions either side of the track. We are to deploy immediately should the frogs decide to advance before dawn. Now go rouse the men and prepare them for duty.'

Newell stormed off in a fury.

'He'll be back to beat me senseless,' said the woman.

It was then he recognized Christina Jenkins. *A pretty thing indeed*, Jonathan thought with emerald green eyes and beautiful raven hair that seemed remarkably well cared for considering the appalling conditions soldiers' women were forced to endure.

Jonathan offered his arm, helping Christina to her feet. Her eyes flooded with tears. Of course Jonathan knew of Will's death, but had yet to find time to comfort the grieving widow. Many officers simply wouldn't have bothered, but Jonathan felt his duty was not only to his men, but to their families if possible.

'Mrs Jenkins, I know words cannot express the grief you must be feeling. I can only say how sorry I am for your lost husband. He was a solid solder with an excellent record…'

'Thank you for your kind words, sir. I do not know what I shall do now I am without support and with a babe on the way. Sergeant Newell wants me for his woman, but it cannot be sir. I cannot see my way to such a man.'

'Is that what all the fuss was about?' Jonathan asked.

'Aye, sir. I believe beating womenfolk pleases him. He wants to claim me with my poor Will dead only a few hours past. He says he has the right. Says I'm denying him the natural order of things. But how can I? He has no right to treat me so.'

'I agree,' Jonathan said. 'We shall have to see Sergeant Newell does not take liberties where his advances are unwelcome.'

'I know a woman cannot survive alone, especially now I am expecting. Sergeant Newell thinks he owns me by right of military rank. He has always had eyes for me. But how can I agree to anything so soon — and I will not accept just anyone. I know I must be practical and in time there will be plenty who'd have me I daresay, but none will challenge Newell now.'

'Well, I can keep him busy for tonight at least, perhaps he will calm down tomorrow,' Jonathan said. 'But rest assured I will not permit him to mistreat you.'

Christina nodded, wringing her hands in her pinafore.

'Allow the other wives to care for you for now,' Jonathan said, taking a guinea from his waistcoat pocket and pressing it into her trembling palm. 'This will last a while until we can decide what is to become of you. I can always arrange for you to be repatriated to England. Do you have family?'

'My dad is the Vicar of Cerne Abbas, sir.'

'I cannot say what tomorrow will bring, Mrs Jenkins. 'Who knows what the Frenchies have up their sleeve? But as soon as can be I shall arrange safe passage for you to England.'

'Thank you, sir, I'll not forget your kindness,' she whispered. 'That's a promise.'

And she kept her word…

Chapter 6 — Refugees

Despite her profound grief, Christina was given little time to dwell. She joined the other women and soldiers to bring rations, more ammunition and water from the supply carts still parked on the river road. In the end she collapsed exhausted along with everyone else. There was nothing more to be done until morning, so she slept under a wagon by the riverbed.

In any event from what Sergeant Newell had said, there was little of poor Will to recover. Christina would pack up their meager traps in the morning and decide what was to be done. Who knew? There was still a battle to be fought…

She awoke at daybreak to the crackle of musketry from the ridgeline. Copious gun-smoke already drifted down the hillside into the river valley. The other women were also awake, but uncertain what to do next.

'All the spare power and shot have been taken aloft,' Mary Boyle said. 'Best we wait by the surgeon's tent. There'll be nursing aplenty if I don't miss my guess.'

As the morning progressed the gunfire appeared to move westwards, eventually fading altogether. The vacuum of silence was unnerving, yet the women were riveted to the spot with doubt and trepidation.

Their indecision was broken when one of the battalion medical orderlies approached.

'Surgeon major's compliments, ma'am,' he addressed Mary who was the camp-followers' unofficial leader. ''E's asked if you ladies will accompany me up the 'ill. There'll be wounded to bring down and no doubt of that. Right now we're short 'anded and any 'elp is much appreciated.'

Major Caldecott, the battalion surgeon had yet to be tested, but the omens were not promising. He was a slovenly man prone to drink and blasphemy and had done little so far other than lance boils and prescribe potions for diarrhoea and sunburn.

Christina had seen the surgeon's tent conditions which did not inspire confidence. Her mother always preached cleanliness and hearty home-cooked meals were the answer to a long healthy life. It was unlikely Caldecott's surgery provided either.

So the women trudged back uphill where a trail of dead and wounded soldiers lay along the ridge. It soon became clear the French brigade had reached the top and driven 2nd Battalion westwards by sheer weight of numbers. It did appear the British troops had withdrawn in good order and casualties were mostly Frenchmen.

Mercifully the French lancers were unable to take advantage of the retreat. The ridge was simply too narrow for them to harry effectively. They were now advancing along the plain hoping to find an opportunity to attack the British flank.

While the other women helped men to the surgeon, Christina and Mary ventured down the gully trail where Jonathan's platoon had been deployed as skirmishers.

The position had been overrun.

Most of the platoon was dead, although it looked as if some men had escaped and reached the main battalion. Christina picked through the rocks, inspecting each man, but none drew breath. Where Will's remains now lay was a mystery. In a way she was grateful, as she had no wish to see what would only be a pile of scarlet pulp.

She spotted a redcoat with sergeant's chevrons sewn to his sleeve. Sergeant Newell showed no signs of life, but French bodies around him indicated he'd fought fiercely and taken several enemy soldiers with him. Bully he may have been, but Sergeant Newell was no coward and fell at the end of a bayonet in a clash of cold steel.

The throb of fly-swarms and squawking crows filled the air and it was only by chance Christina heard a groan from behind a boulder. She discovered Lieutenant McAlister crumpled with his uniform drenched in blood. He had a musket ball in his leg and shoulder.

Christina found Jonathan's pistol, reloaded it and stuck the weapon into her pinafore pocket. She also shouldered a satchel of powder and lead balls. She had an uneasy feeling she'd need some fire-power before too much longer. Mary gathered a musket and two bayonets, one of which she gave to Christina.

Mary helped Christina drag Jonathan from the battlefield.

''E won't live if that sot, Caldecott gets 'is 'and on 'im,' Mary surmised.

'But what can we do?'

'Take care 'of 'im ourselves, lovely,' Mary said grimly. 'Don't rightly know where me 'ubby is just now so we'll just 'ave to make do. That sawbones is gonna be too busy to be bothered with the likes of us. 'E's too lazy anyway.'

And then a medical orderly showed up.

'Still alive, is 'e?' the orderly said, eyeing Jonathan with little confidence. 'We'd better get 'im down to the surgeon then. I reckon that leg'll 'ave to go. Arm too most likely.'

Christina was appalled, but that was the general treatment of the time — got a bullet in it, chop it off!

She drew the pistol and told the orderly to leave.

'But he's our officer,' the man protested.

'Well, he is *my* officer now,' she said with a menace that could not be ignored. 'Do not think I cannot use this gun. A parson's daughter I may be, but I have been around soldiers long enough to put a ball between your eyes!'

The orderly scampered away. One half dead lieutenant wasn't worth the risk of being shot.

In any event the custodial problem was settled shortly afterwards.

It took some time for Christina and Mary to haul Jonathan back to the River Tagus. By then Surgeon Major Caldecott — fearful of being left behind to French mercy — had loaded the wounded onto all the available mule-drawn wagons before following the river westwards. Obviously lieutenants guarded by rambunctious females were expendable.

Christina, Mary and Jonathan were now abandoned. Although several handcarts remained, much of the battalion provisions were gone.

The first job was to clean and dress Jonathan's wounds. He was barely conscious, which was just as well because Christina gouged the balls from his wounds with a bayonet point. Even so it took all Mary's strength to hold Jonathan down as he writhed in agony.

Next Christina carefully picked the wadded shreds of uniform material from the wounds to avoid infection. Jonathan rested afterwards, but he breathed so shallowly, it was difficult to tell if he was still alive. One of Christina's few luxuries was a hand-mirror which she placed close to Jonathan's face and was relieved to see condensation form on the glass.

Meanwhile even though it seemed the battalion had cleaned out most of its supplies, Mary had been scavenging around the camp and gathered enough food, water bags, wine, blankets and weapons for the three of them. Christina recovered Jonathan's money pouch containing several guineas. She replaced the coin Jonathan had given her and put the purse in her pinafore pocket.

Mary eyed her suspiciously.

'We will have need of money, Mary. I have but a few coppers and I would say a corporal's wife is not better funded.'

Mary nodded with a wry smile.

'It ain't like thievin' if we use the dosh to keep 'imself alive.'

Christina nodded.

'I daresay an officer's sovereigns will stretch further when negotiated by soldiers' women,' she grinned.

'What now?' Mary sighed, crouching on her haunches while gulping from a wine bladder before handing it to Christina.

She wasn't much of a drinker and had barely tasted wine before as cider and ale were the Cerne Abbas tipples of choice, but Christina drank heartily.

'I think we should stay put and let Mr McAlister rest today and see how he is in the morning,' Christina said. 'Then I fancy we will have to load him into one of these carts with as much food as we can carry and head west.'

'I wonder if we'll catch up with the army,' Mary said.

'Who knows? Perhaps we will have to trudge all the way back to the coast.'

They considered that prospect for a short time and then built a fire as the day drew into afternoon. They boiled water and brewed tea, which had become popular and affordable recently thanks to the East India Company playing dirty tricks in China and the sub-continent. But the British government turned a blind eye because tea was big business and provided a bountiful cash-flow to the exchequer coffers.

'Thank you for staying, Mary,' Christina said. 'You could have most likely caught up with the others.'

'I couldn't leave you out here alone, me little treasure. You're a decent lass 'oo's just lost 'er man and still you're tryin' to 'elp. And this lad being so poorly. My Alf — wherever 'e might be — says Mr McAlister is a right gent when some of them officers are just trumped-up toffs. It ain't proper to leave you two in the lurch.'

'Mr McAlister showed me much kindness when Sergeant Newell bullied me.'

'Aye, that Newell ain't no sad loss.'

'Alas, I cannot think of anything else I can do for Mr McAlister at this moment.'

'Me neither. We'll manage somehow.'

So they spent the night comfortably enough. They collected ample fuel for the fire where they baked damper and ate sausages, lentils and dried fruit. They brewed some broth for Jonathan, but it mostly dribbled down his chin.

'Sleep's what 'e needs,' Mary opined. 'We'll see if 'e's up for some grub tomorrow.'

The night passes peacefully, only interrupted by Jonathan's groans when he rolled in his sleep. On these occasions Christina and Mary checked his wounds and dripped water through his lips. No one passed by, so it seemed the local population had fled the warring armies.

But that was not the way things remained.

At dawn, while Mary kept a weather eye along the road, Christina prepared breakfast, which was much the same as supper.

'...'ello, what's that?' Mary murmured between clenched teeth. 'Grab your pistol, love. I think we've got company.'

Half a dozen ragged individuals stalked cautiously towards the women's campsite. They were armed with pistols, cutlasses, knives and muskets. Their clothing was patched cotton fabric and each man wore a broad-brimmed sombrero.

'Bandits..?' Christina ventured.

'If that's the case, we're in big trouble.'

The men approached cautiously, stopping abruptly when they noticed a pair of women in their path.

Mary raised her musket before the strangers had time to aim their guns.

'That's close enough!' she declared with rather more authority than she had the firepower to enforce, although Christina had also leveled her pistol towards the newcomers as well.

The men exchanged glances, and chattered to one another in rapid Spanish. Suddenly they all burst into laughter.

'What's so bleedin' funny?' Mary demanded.

'I do not think they understand English,' Christina observed.

The men inched forward.

Mary cocked the musket. She had gathered other guns, but they rested against the handcart where Jonathan lay. Effectively Mary and Christina had just two shots before the rogues were upon them.

'If it's thievin', rape and murder you have in mind, we ain't gonna be easy,' Mary challenged, but as the advancing men didn't appear to understand. She was wasting her breath.

As they closed in the men drew their pistols and knives menacingly.

Mary shot the leading man through the heart, while Christina hit another man in the gut. As the smoke cleared the men charged, screaming hysterically. Mary brandished the bayonet and Christina drew a knife from her skirts, but their attackers now had loaded pistols at the ready.

Then a shot blasted from behind Christina. One of the bandits shrieked as blood and bone splinters sprayed from his knee. Seconds later another shot rang out and a fourth attacker pitched forward into the dust and lay still.

As the remaining bandits jerked to a halt, Christina glanced behind to see Jonathan's prone body beside two spent muskets. The effort of grabbing and firing the weapons was all he could manage before lapsing into unconsciousness once more.

The fleeing bandits didn't get far.

A group of armed horsemen galloped from the west into their midst and cut the thieves to pieces with their swords.

'Bleedin' 'ell,' Mary muttered, 'we're in deep bleedin' shit now.'

The oncoming riders galloped on with bare breaking stride to finish off the bandits. They were a dozen of them. Bronzed mustachioed men and a couple of raven-haired women who rode beside the leading rider dressed in a scarlet jacket, tight cavalry pants and gleaming leather boots. He wore a tasseled shako held in place with a chin-strap.

There was nothing Christina or Mary could do but watch the riders as they reined to a halt in front of them. There was no time to run away and nowhere to hide anyway.

The redcoat doffed his shako inclining his head slightly.

'Top of the mornin' to you, ladies,' he greeted in a soft pleasant Scottish accent.

'Thank you for arriving just in time, sir,' Christina said.

'A pleasure to be of service, indeed. Allow me to introduce myself…'

'I recognise you, sir,' Christina said. 'You are the officer who joined our battalion at Talavera.'

'Absolutely, Major Colquhoun Grant. My colleagues are Portuguese partisans who have joined me to spy on the froggies for General Wellesley. To whom do I have the honour of addressing?'

'I am Christina Jenkins and this is Mary Boyle. We are soldiers' wives. I fear I am a widow now, but we know not of Mary's husband's whereabouts.'

'He may yet be safe, ma'am,' Grant said to Mary. 'The battalion retired in good order and finally drove the frogs away. They will have reached the main force at Almaraz by now.'

'We have a poorly officer, sir,' Christina said. 'We tend him as best we know, but I fear he is in a sad state.'

Grant dismounted while Christina and Mary returned Jonathan to his bedroll.

'He has heart, sir,' Christina said. 'He was shot twice upon that hill. We have taken the lead from his arm and leg. He has been unconscious since, yet woke long enough to fire two muskets at those villains just now.'

'Ah, young McAlister if I am not mistaken,' Grant said.

'Yes sir, he was my Will's platoon officer. Will was killed by cannon shot in yesterday's fight.'

'My condolence, ma'am,' Grant said with what seemed to Christina genuine sincerity.

'We plan to take the officer west in one of these 'and carts,' Mary added.

'Most commendable indeed,' Grant replied, 'but I fear Mr. McAlister is unlikely to survive such a journey and I doubt he'll have full use of that gun-shot leg even if he recovers.'

'We cannot leave him here like that wretched Major Caldecott,' Christina declared.

'I fear you may misjudge Caldecott, ma'am. We passed him along the road. He is trying to get the wounded back to Almaraz which he just might do in the nick of time.'

'I suppose the major has differing priorities,' Christina acknowledged grudgingly.

'Quite,' Grant said.

He addressed one of the women in his group. After a brief discussion he returned to where Mary and Christina nursed Jonathan's.

'Danilo and Estela will escort you to a farmhouse nearby,' Grant said. 'The owners are no friends of France. It will be best for

McAlister to recover there until he regains strength enough to travel further.'

'Thank you sir, you have been most kind,' Christina said, even bobbing a dainty curtsy.

'Think nothing of it, ma'am,' Grant replied graciously. 'But I admonish you not to tarry a moment longer than possible. I understand General Wellesley plans to regroup to the west in Portugal leaving the froggies to grow bolder in Spain.'

'Thank you, sir. We hope to reach the coast directly.'

'And now I must bid you good day, ladies. We shall scour yonder battle ground and recover ordnance for the partisans to take the fight to the French.'

Grant touched his shako peak, remounted and led his partisans up to the ridge top.'

'Come,' Estela said urgently. 'We go now.'

With Danilo's help they laid Jonathan on the largest cart, before gathering any spare blankets, food and water and loading it aboard. They stuffed anything else into abandoned military knapsacks they hitched over their shoulders. When they'd gleaned all they could, Estela hitched her horse to the dray. The animal didn't find the situation appealing, but Estela stood no nonsense from the beast.

They reached the stone cottage around noon. It was a pleasant enough building close to the river just above the flood line and shaded by a giant elm tree. However, prosperity wasn't widespread these days. If the French and Spanish hadn't stolen what they could find, Wellesley's foragers cleaned up anything remaining.

The farm belonged to Danilo's aunt and uncle who weren't particularly enthusiastic about harbouring a military fugitive. The

French and Spanish were notorious for bullying innocent civilians for no good reason, let alone aiding and comforting the enemy.

Estela and Danilo didn't linger. After a brief introduction to the farmers, Jesenia and Nazario, they mounted and galloped off to join Grant. The elderly couple spoke no English, so most communications were done by grunts and sign language.

And so they waited for Jonathan McAlister to recover...

Chapter 7 — Moving On

Sadly, Jonathan didn't recover as Christina had hoped. At first she was optimistic as she cleaned Jonathan's wounds, but infection set in, swelling into areas of yellow pus. Jonathan rallied when Christina lanced the canker and washed the scarred area. But the infection always returned and Jonathan lapsed into feverish semi-consciousness.

She and Mary tended him until early autumn and the elm leaves was beginning to turn yellow and float to earth. As yet there was no sign of the British Army, but the French prowled around. Several cavalry troops passed by, scrounging what little was left. So far Christina and Mary were warned in time — old Nazario was so attuned to the land he farmed, he sensed anything new.

They hid with Jonathan in a nearby cave, which the French showed no inclination to explore. Nazario and Jesenia stored their winter provisions there, which they'd harvested despite French, British and Spanish pillaging. They also hid two penned hogs and a chicken coop with several laying hens.

After a time the patrols rode by as word apparently spread there was nothing left to steal. But as the weather grew colder and the days shortened Christina became nervous that troops might use the farmhouse as a warm billet and there would be no way of going undetected then.

'It's time to move on,' she told Mary. 'We'll have to take our chances with the French.'

But they'd left it too late…

*

Frost lay on the ground at dawn and a blue smoke haze hovered around the farmhouse as Jesenia added another log to the kitchen embers. As usual Nazario heard the hoof beats long before riders appeared.

'Go!' he urged Christina who roused Mary and they were able to drag Jonathan away just as a squadron of French dragoons thundered along the river valley.

Christina didn't witness what occurred, but she heard the cavalry ride away about an hour later. Normally Jesenia or Nazario would come for them once the coast was clear, but on this occasion no one came.

By noon Jonathan was shivering and Christina knew she must take him to the fire for warmth or he would die.

It may have been prudent to reconnoiter first, but it took both women to help Jonathan back to the farmhouse. They lugged him through the back door and placed him beside the fire, which had all but burnt out.

Mary and Christina exchanged puzzled glances. It seemed the French had gone, but Jesenia and Nazario were nowhere to be seen either.

'Maybe they've gone to the vegetable patch...' Mary suggested.

'Why? The French will have picked it clean.'

Christina edged the front door ajar and peered through.

'Oh dear God,' she gasped. 'How could they have done this..?'

'What?' Mary said irritably.

Christina opened the door fully. Shadows swayed across the front porch. The old farm couple dangled from two stout elm branches. It was obvious Christina and Mary were not in time to save them.

'The bastards!' Mary spat followed by a string of barrack room expletives.

'Quickly, we must cut them down.'

As they did so they saw a note attached to each corpse. The paper wasn't pinned to their clothes, but hammered in with garden nails. Blood stains suggested Jesenia and Nazario were still alive when the spikes had been driven home. Mercifully Christina and Mary were beyond earshot and didn't hear the screams.

After they retrieved the nails and laid the bodies beside each other, Christina examined the notes written in Spanish.

Both women had picked up a little rudimentary Spanish, but neither could interpret the message.

'I wonder what it says..?' Christina though aloud.

'This is the punishment for those who help partisans,' a voice spoke softly from behind them.

Christina and Mary spun around to confront Major Grant, who'd approached so quietly they hadn't sensed his presence. He looked careworn and not his usual dapper self.

'How could the French be so cruel?' Christian wept. 'They were just two innocent old people.'

'It seems the French thought otherwise,' Grant sighed with resignation.

'Surely they did not know of Mr McAlister and us. And we are not partisans in any event.'

'Indeed that is most likely so,' Grant conceded, 'but it may have much to do with a French reconnaissance patrol ambushed about ten miles away.'

'What does that have to do with anything?' Mary said.

'The partisans killed most of the soldiers in the fight, but captured a few, pegged them to the ground before castrating them and leaving them to bleed to death.'

Christina stood speechless.

'Yes, ma'am this war has generated a new kind of hatred and barbarity. I fear the cycle will continue. But I thought you would have been long away by now.'

'Mr McAlister does not respond well, sir,' Christina said. 'I clean the canker from his wounds for it only to return. He has yet to gain the strength to fight the malady. Some days he is barely conscious.'

'I suggest we move him anyway. The French have cut off any chance of joining Wellington's main force to the north.'

'Wellington? Has General Wellesley been replaced?'

Grant chuckled.

'Of course you would not have heard. Our esteemed leader is no longer merely Arthur Wellesley, but has been awarded a peerage — Viscount Wellington of Talavera!'

'That might be very nice for 'is lordship, considerin' it weren't a case of who won, but who lost least. An' while I'm 'appy as anyone for 'im,' Mary said. 'But 'ow the bleedin' 'ell do we get past them froggies?'

'Eloquently and astutely put, Mrs Boyle,' Grant replied.

Christina shouldn't have been surprised he remembered their names.   Major Colquhoun Grant didn't strike her a man who forgot much. Exploring officers were expected to keep all they saw in their heads and not rely on documents which could be captured by enemy troops.

'We will travel south. There are highland trails that lead west into Portugal.'

'We..?' Christina ventured.

'Indeed, ma'am. I cannot in all conscience leave two ladies and a wounded comrade to the mercy of our foe. But we must make haste. The French will not await our convenience. Gather food, water and as much to keep you warm as you can carry.'

'What 'appened to them other partisans?' Mary asked.

'I left them to their butchery a fortnight ago,' Grant explained. 'I have been gathering intelligence since and have much to relate to his lordship.'

'More importantly what about poor Jesenia and Nazario?' Christina said. 'We surely cannot leave them where they lie.'

'Alas we must. We will cover their bodies and others will come in time.'

'You will guide us to Lisbon, sir?' Christina ventured.

'Much of the way no doubt,' Grant replied. 'I must take the circumspect route myself as the French may lie in ambush between here and Wellington's Army. I have important information to impart, although I do not predict a major campaign before next spring.'

So they took the high trails south and west while the French rampaged unchecked through northern Spain. Winter crept onwards and snow now covered the higher peaks. Fortunately they carried enough food for a month because there was little to be found in the high country. There was even less available in the plains as Wellington had ordered his army to confiscate all they could carry and burn what was left.

Tens of thousands of peasants and villagers were relocated closer to Lisbon.

They were a week upon the high trails during which time Christina's healthy baby girl was born. Christina was young and fit and was blessed with a quick and relatively easy delivery. The birth slowed their progress some, but in time they reached Lisbon little the worse for wear other than cuts, bruises and sore feet.

There had been two small but sharp clashes with deserters who were seen off after a few warning shots, while some astute bribes were needed to satisfy avaricious Portuguese officials.

Mary Boyle was a woman who'd marched behind Wellington's Army for years with several battalions so she wasn't daunted by what she considered merely a short walk. Christina stoically followed her example.

'Delightful as your company has been, ladies, I fear I must report to Wellington's headquarters,' Grant said when they finally reached the city. 'I suggest you take young McAlister to the nearest medical ship moored at the Port of Lisbon.'

'Thank you for all your kindness, sir,' Christina said. 'I do not think we would have arrived here if not for you.'

'I would not be so sure,' Grant smiled. 'You seem like resourceful ladies to me.'

'I 'ate to let you down, but I'll 'ave to leave you too, luv,' Mary said.

'I know, Mary. You have to discover what has become of your Alf. I will pray that you find him safe.'

Meanwhile Grant accosted two soldiers who seemed to have no meaningful work to do at present. The men snapped to attention. Grant questioned them about their unit discovering they were on two days leave and had spent all their pay in town.

'Right, here's a silver florin for each of you to escort Mrs Jenkins and this wounded officer to the nearest hospital ship.'

The men eyed the silver coins. They couldn't believe their luck. The Port of Lisbon was close by and here was enough cash to stay drunk all day.

'Now I know your names and your units so I shall know where to find you if I hear you have not fulfilled your duty.'

'Oh, you can count on us, sir. We won't let you down.'

Grant mounted his horse and turned to Mary, extending his arm.

'Come Mrs Doyle. Ride behind me and we will endeavour to track down your battalion. Farewell Mrs Jenkins. You are a woman of pluck and it has been a pleasure to make your acquaintance. Good luck to you and Mr McAlister. God speed.'

Christina waved goodbye as Grant and Mary disappeared through the narrow streets seething with soldiers, sailors, marines, local hawkers and street walkers, where gentry rubbed shoulders with ne'er-do-wells.

'This way missus,' one of the redcoats who introduced himself as 'Arold said. 'We'll pull the cart for you. The wharf is a rough spot, but don't fret. You won't come to harm if Jimmie and me 'ave anything to say about it.'

In time they reached the Port of Lisbon where a Royal Navy hospital ship lay bound for Tisbury Dock.

'Would you like us to help you get the young officer aboard, missus?' Harold asked Christina.

'Please wait with Mr McAlister, gentlemen,' Christina said. 'I shall be but a moment.'

'Dunno as we're gents, missus,' Jimmie grinned. 'But don't worry. One thing we knows and that's 'ow to follow orders and Major Grant was most insistent.'

Christina's doubts were proven correct. No one challenged her as she walked up one of the gangplanks. The ship was an ancient third-rater which had seen service in the American Revolution. The entrance Christina chose by mere chance led to a hatch on the third deck. The gun-decks were cleared to make room for wounded soldiers.

The stench of, sweat, human waste and purification was so rank Christina gagged and tied her scarf over her nose and mouth, which did little good. The sight even in dim candlelight was equally appalling. Men lay in cramped rows either on the deck or in abutting hammocks.

Most casualties were missing limbs while blood and pus seeped through their bandages. Once Christina grew used to the fetid atmosphere she became aware of a continuous buzzing groan from the suffering men punctuated by pitiful wails of pain and distress.

Oh dear God, this is even worse than the battlefield. This is truly hell!

'May I be of assistance, ma'am?' a fellow who Christina took to be a surgeon by the look of his blood-stained apron.

'I believe not, thank you sir,' Christian replied. 'I have a wounded man in my care, but I fear he will not do well aboard this ship.'

'Indeed, ma'am, if you think this is bad I invite you to inspect the orlop.'

Christina stared at him blankly.

'The lower deck where operations are performed,' the surgeon explained. 'We bring the patients to the upper two decks afterwards.'

Christina was so appalled by the squalor and overcrowding she wondered if anyone would survive the voyage, or indeed, whether the ship would sail at all. So, to Harold and Jimmie's dismay, she bade the surgeon good day, but refused to put Jonathan aboard and began searching for alternatives.

'But, missus, a sailor just told us this is the last 'ospital ship sailin' for a week,' Harold pleaded. 'Major Grant will 'ave our 'ides if we don't do like 'e told us.'

Harold wasn't exaggerating either. Disobeying a direct order was a flogging offence in both army and navy.

'I will not tell him if you help me find accommodation until I can secure a more suitable passage. When we set sail Major Grant will be none the wiser. Take a look inside that demonic abomination if you think I am doing wrong,' Christina pointed to the deck-hatch. 'Those poor souls aboard are in abject torment.'

Money was becoming scarce and accommodation scarcer, but eventually she rented a cheap hotel room. After thanking Harold and Jimmie for their patience Christina said goodbye before making the room habitable with tenacious use of a broom and mop.

The city was total, boisterous chaos and finding a ship was more than just walking along the docks. There were vessels bound for Gibraltar, the Mediterranean, the Canaries, Thames ports and even America, but all were either full or their masters unwilling to carry a woman with a new-born baby and a wounded man. In desperation Christina left Jonathan and her daughter in the care of a friendly chambermaid and roamed the dockside streets and taverns vainly searching for a ship to carry them home.

She was still unsuccessful by nightfall. Even armed with Jonathan's pistol, the streets were too dangerous for a lone woman to be aboard after dark. So she decided to return to the hotel to tend Jonathan and feed her infant.

Approaching a corner close to the hotel she saw three men waylay a victim and beat him to the ground. Without a thought she drew the pistol from her pinafore pocket, aimed and fired, hitting one of the rogues in his leg. He yelped and limped off. Fortunately his companions followed, because she had no idea what she would have done against three footpads armed with only a discharged pistol.

The fallen man was in bad shape. Blood flowed from his head and he moaned in a semi-conscious state. She was able to hoist him to his feet and together they limped back to Christina's room. He collapsed to the floor and lay still where she bathed his wounds and folded his coat under his head as a pillow.

'Wonderful!' she sighed at the sight of two bodies lying crammed in that tiny room. 'Now I have three to care for.'

Her baby cried, she was hungry and settled to Christina's breast.

'God love you, what good girl you are, only complaining when there is need,' she crooned. 'I have not even named you yet. How can a mother have so little time not to name her baby?'

'Call her Natalie Jane,' mumbled the wounded man from the floor.

'Why so?' asked Christina, but he had lapsed into sleep again.

The chambermaid brought Christina a spicy soup, rough-grained bread and two oranges. She spooned a little soup through Jonathan's lips and finished the rest eagerly with some sausage left over from her rations. The chambermaid insisted she squeeze some orange juice for Jonathan and eat the rest indicating with signs-language that oranges helped fight infection and stopped bleeding gums.

By morning Christina's second burden seemed much recovered although in a foul mood. He cursed and swore which Christina allowed was better than anything she had heard in the battalion barracks over the last year.

'My, my, are you not the happy one this fine morning?' she said offering a cup of tea she'd brought from the hotel kitchen.

'Woman, you have robbed me blind and beaten me half senseless. How do you expect me to feel?' he blazed, but accepted the tea.

'Not me, but those rascals who well had the better of you. How foolish you are to roam these streets at night and fall prey to foot-pads.'

He smiled a little. He was a man of middle age, bearded and muscular to the point where Christina wondered how he could have been waylaid so effectively.

'Drink and women!' he declared. 'It's a sailor's lot to fall foul of 'em. Addles his brain and senses, and no doubt of that! But it's a long time at sea and a short time ashore, so a man must make what he can of it.'

'I agree with you about drink, but a good woman can be a man's saviour,' Christina said primly.

'I didn't say anything about "good women", lass.'

'Do you have a name?' Christina asked.

'Barnaby Grogan, at your service ma'am,' he replied, and it was about then that he noticed Jonathan lying so close by. 'And to whom do I have the honour of addressing?'

'Oh, I'm Christina,' she replied. 'And you named my baby last night.'

He showed no surprise but then rolled his eyes in Jonathan's direction as if to ask a question.

She hesitated for just a moment.

'He's my husband. I'm Mrs. McAlister!'

It was so sudden she even shocked herself. Why had she said that? Had it been for protection? A married woman in Lisbon was no safer than any other unless her husband was strong enough to protect her. Was it because of the baby? She had been properly wed so there was no shame in her conception. Jonathan had been kind to her once, was she just dreaming?

Grogan seemed to accept her story. It turned out that he was first mate on a cargo vessel presently loading salted sardines for Weymouth.

Christina's heart leapt, she wasn't going to let this opportunity pass. At first Grogan was reluctant, but she finally persuaded him to take them on board.

'I'm only taking you because you saved my first mate and I'd be hard pressed to replace him afore we cast off,' the captain growled when Grogan brought them on board. 'You'll serve as maid and scullion to pay your passage — and I don't want to 'ear no moanin' about the smell o' sardines!'

The voyage was cold but fair, and although she worked hard, she enjoyed the sea and salt air. Her baby thrived and was never sea sick, although Jonathan fared less well. He grew weaker and had trouble even keeping water down as they sailed for Weymouth.

But, arrive they did and once on dry land Jonathan rallied. The sea air and salt water seemed to retard his infection. After landing at Weymouth's North Quay it was an easy task to hire a carriage for the short journey to Cerne Abbas. Especially as the Reverend Cornelius Proud, Christina's popular and much respected father would pay the fare. So accompanied by a convalescing officer and her baby, Christina travelled to her parent's home.

Chapter 8 — Homecoming

The pastor and his good wife were overwhelmed to see their daughter safe and sound. The news of young Will Jenkins' death had long reached them, but they'd heard nothing of his wife.

Christina's mother, Emma Proud took Jonathan in hand and with a mixture of good old-fashioned rural know-how, efficacious herbal remedies and cleanliness, further infection was averted. With rest Jonathan began the road to recovery more quickly than anyone had hoped. He was soon tentatively up and about, and of course, Christina was there to nurse him every step of the way.

It was obvious Jonathan's leg would never be as before and he would henceforth always walk with a limp. Christina bought him a stout blackthorn shillelagh which helped his balance considerably.

It was also time for Jonathan to decide what to do about his military career. Technically he was absent without leave, but after writing to Whitehall explaining the situation was beyond his control their lordships were uncharacteristically understanding. They granted Jonathan leave without pay and suggested he sell his commission as he was unlikely to fulfil his duties as an infantry officer in the future.

Jonathan was in no hurry to make such decisions and content to remain at Cerne Abbas with Christina.

By degrees the young couple fell in love. Not passionately at first, rather through common interests and a cheerful, optimistic outlook on life. But as their love deepened Christina knew she would soon come **to** Jonathan's bed. A situation that was not lost on Reverend and Mrs. Proud! Indeed the good cleric was just the man best qualified to do something about it.

Wedding banns were posted without delay!

'Should we not tell your family?' Christina asked.

'I think not,' replied Jonathan. 'Explaining to mother is more than I'm prepared to do for now. If you wish we can reaffirm our vows at a big ceremony, if that is what everyone wants. Let's just do this for us! I don't want to wait.'

And so it was on a beautiful crisp winter morning in a quiet country church Christina and Jonathan were married. It was a bigger affair than she expected, attended by a large part of Cornelius Proud's congregation. Even Will's family turned up to wish the bride and groom well. They were pragmatic folk who mourned Will's death, but understood life went on and no one could resent Christina's future happiness. Afterwards everyone crammed into the cosy pub for hearty spit roast accompanied by enough cider and beer for all. Reverend Pound even broke out kegs of his prized contraband claret and brandy.

'I would like to have a big family,' Christina declared some days later as they were taking a late afternoon ride in the family trap. 'Lots of girls and lots of boys!'

'I don't mind at all,' Jonathan laughed.

'And I know just the place to start,' she giggled. 'The Fertility Giant on the hill. Let's go there tonight?'

'What's wrong with right now?' he said and urged their horse into a fast trot.

Carved in the chalk centuries before and maintained through the generations the giant was easy to spot against the green grazing meadows in which it lay. There was no doubt to its symbolism.

'I feel a little inadequate compared to that chap,' Jonathan conceded.

'I am sure you will do very well,' Christina said with a wink as they collapsed onto the grass in the centre of the monument. Jonathan's leg still pained him and he leant on the shillelagh for support. They were both a little breathless after the hill climb and lay in each other's arms for a moment. Couples had come here for ages hoping to enhance their chances of becoming parents.

But lovemaking was not to be…

'Well, lookee here,' an icy voice sneered. 'Mr-'igh-'n-bleedin'-mighty Lieutenant McAlister if I ain't mistaken. And all cosy-cosy with 'is whore, what's not good enough for us lowly soldiers!'

Scrambling to their feet they met Sergeant Newell climbing the hill and only yards away.

'Newell! You're supposed to be dead!' Jonathan stammered realising as he spoke how foolish it must have sounded.

'Well obviously not!' Newell roared. 'Takes more than a scratch from French steel to put me down. I was out for a bit, but I got back to Lisbon all on me own dodgin' patrols and bleeding renegades all the way.'

'How did you find us?' Christina asked. She could not stop shaking for Newell was a fearful sight in his rage and jealously.

'Oh, that was easy. See I 'ad a nice chat with Mary Boyle before she found 'er 'ubby. She told me all about 'ow you and 'er and that poncy spy got to the coast. Happy to save a bleedin' pansy officer, but left me for dead.'

'I checked,' Christina stammered. 'I was sure there was no sign of life.'

'Didn't check 'ard enough seems to me.'

Christina almost thought of apologising, but Newell didn't give the chance.

'Army thought I was still too sick for duty, so they sent me back to Yeovil on a pox-ridden 'ospital ship. Got wind o' what you was up to from the barracks adjutant. Weren't 'ard to find you from there.'

'And what precisely do you want, Newell?' Jonathan demanded.

'Why I wan 'er, you blitherin' fool!' Newell bellowed. 'She's mine and I aim to 'ave her.'

'I was never yours Jack Newell,' Christina screamed. 'Never! Never! And I never will be. I am Jonathan's wife now!'

'I'm afraid she's right,' Jonathan said reasonably, trying to calm everyone down. 'You see we were married a few days ago. So, please turn around and be on your way, there's a good fellow.'

'On my bleedin' way!' Newell's face grew scarlet with anger. 'You've finished pushing me around, so you 'ave!'

Without warning Newell charged. He cannoned into Jonathan knocking the wind out of him. In fact Jonathan would have been no match for Newell fully fit, but his wounds placed him at a hopeless disadvantage. He fought back as best he could, but Newell's fists rained down mercilessly and soon his face was bloody and bruised from the punches.

'Get off him!' Christina screamed, realising in seconds that words would be of no use.

It was instinct she told herself later. She grabbed Jonathan's shillelagh and brought the weighted end crashing onto Newell's skull. She struck him again and again, long after he went limp and slumped forward. She'd lost one husband and no one was going to rob her of another, least of all scum like Newell.

Jonathan finally managed to crawl clear and took the bloody stick from her hands. She clung to him as they staggered down the hill to the trap.

'It's not your fault, it's not your fault,' he crooned, but she was still sobbing uncontrollably when they reached the parsonage.

Emma Proud put Christina to bed and stayed to nurse her. She was a no-nonsense woman, and took the situation in her stride.

'Well, well,' the equally unflappable reverend said, 'what must we do about this unfortunate state of affairs?'

'We must tell the authorities. It was self-defence. Christina saved my life.' Jonathan said. 'Again,' he added in a whisper.

'Now that may not be for the best,' Proud continued. 'Sheriff Lightfoot is certainly a fair and reasonable man, but he and Will Jenkins have history which might influence his attitude towards Christina.'

'We cannot just leave Newell where he lies.'

'Indeed not, but this will take some unravelling. And you will have to return to your battalion at some time even if you eventually sell your commission. Killing one of its sergeants, however justified the circumstances, will hardly further your career. Or do any good for anyone. You must think of Christina and the scandal as well.'

'Do you have anything in mind?' Jonathan asked, because for the life of him he couldn't think of an answer.

'We must act on our own,' Reverend Proud declared. 'It's well past dark. It's unlikely anyone has witnessed this sad event or we'd have heard about it by now, so the least we can do is give this rogue a decent, Christian burial. It's probably more than he deserves, but then I am in the forgiveness business, am I not?'

So in the dead of night the trap set off back uphill to the giant chalk carving.

The following morning old Clem Watkins, having died peacefully in his sleep, was laid to rest after eighty-eight years of a fulfilling and hearty life. As the sods covered his coffin no one knew a body wrapped in a white shroud lay beneath. No stranger to hard work, Reverend Proud had dug an extra three feet below the grave where he and Jonathan placed Jack Newell's corpse. After a hasty prayer, they refilled the earth a few inches above the body that now rested below Clem Watkins' casket.

That evening they found Christina much recovered and in a better mood. Over a few glasses of port they swore to secrecy feeling not too guilty, as they believed Sergeant Newell had brought his misfortune upon himself.

'This must be a suitable time to tell your family you are home, Jonathan,' declared the good reverend. 'It will do Christina no harm to be away from here for a while at least.'

And the matter of Sergeant Newell was closed, his disappearance remaining a mystery forever.

*

It was now time for Jonathan to take his bride to meet his parents and Christina was terrified. She had wondered whether Jonathan may have thought her unworthy to meet his titled family, but then why would he have married her — just to bed her? But she knew that wasn't his style otherwise she would never have fallen in love with him.

'Of course I'm proud of you,' Jonathan reassured her. 'Who wouldn't be? You're beautiful, brave, loving, loyal and hard-working. Any man would be delighted to have you as his wife. I am the envy of the world.'

'But I am just a humble country girl.'

'That is nothing to be ashamed of. My great-grandfather was an indentured servant transported to the American colonies as a Jacobite rebel.'

'But you have delayed returning home. Your family must worry.'

In truth Jonathan had written to his parents assuring them he was recovering and he'd be home soon.

'There are two reasons,' he explained.' The first is purely selfish. I am simply enjoying time alone with you and no family pressure.'

'*My* parents are close by.'

'They have a wonderful way of giving us space, darling. I love them for that.'

'And the other reason..?'

'I want to return home fully recovered and not as a cripple.'

'You are not a cripple! You just walk with teeny-weeny limp. That is all.'

'Then it is time to meet the family,' he said, kissing her.

A carriage duly arrived to convey the newlyweds to Glen Briar Hall.

The manor was situated on a sizeable estate an easy carriage ride from the Roman town of Bath, which was a favourite destination for well-heeled gentry to see and be seen. Christina had only been to Bath once on market day and loved the hustle and bustle of elegant folk as they promenaded through cobbled streets sampling the wares.

Jonathan had said little of his parents other than his father had been awarded his knighthood for services during the American Revolutionary War.

'I have no idea how that came about, because we lost that damned scrap and father's brother, my Uncle Fergus, fought on the patriot's side,' Jonathan declared glibly as they rode through the main gate. 'He retained my grandfather William's cotton and tobacco estates in Virginia. Grandfather received a huge land grant after the Seven Year War over fifty years ago.'

'So your father and uncle are no longer friends…?' Christina assumed.

'Oh, quite on the contrary, darling. Uncle Fergus exports cotton to father's Lancashire mills. They do not intend for a little war to get in the way of their friendship and enterprise. They manage handsomely.'

They rode along a gravel road lined with oaks beyond which lay pasture where a variety of livestock grazed. They passed French style formal gardens and orchards approaching the manor house. The flora was neatly pruned awaiting spring's revival. Indeed blue bells already sprouted in profusion.

'There looks like quite a welcoming committee,' Jonathan said as the carriage drew to a halt and a footman opened the coach door.

Sir Monroe and Lady Abigail McAlister stood beside Jonathan's younger sister, Rosemary who looked stunning in a white gown, no bonnet, but with greenhouse reared garlands adorning her hair. If Christina felt anyway inferior, she didn't show it, but calmly took each of the family's hand in turn.

'Charmed, my dear,' Sir Monroe drawled, sounding sincere in Christina's opinion.

'So we meet Jonathan's mysterious new bride. And what an exquisite creature you are, my darling girl,' Lady McAlister announced. 'We hoped our son's wedding would be here at Glen Briar Hall, but not so it seems. You must tell Sir Monroe and me all about yourself.'

'Oh Christina,' Rosemary gushed. 'I know we shall be dear, *dear* friends. We shall have so much fun. It is simply divine to have a sister.'

What a pleasant surprise. They're just so friendly.

'We have invited a few friends to a dinner party in your honour tonight,' Sit Monroe said. 'And we have engaged a small orchestra for a little dancing afterwards. I hope you do not mind.'

'Come, Christina dear,' Lady McAlister said. 'We will show you to your rooms and there is plenty of time to rest and change. I know Nanny has been just dying to take great care of your little one.'

Glen Briar Hall was luxurious but not pretentious. Dinner was served at a long table accommodating about twenty guests in the dining room adjoining the dance floor.

To Christina, standing beside her husband, this was paradise. Footmen swirled back and forth with trays of champagne as the dinner guests assembled and were introduced. A selection of graceful and urbane nobility mingled with several handsome military officers, resplendent in their scarlet and blue uniforms.

Christina sat between Lady McAlister and Rosemary. The table was a bedazzling array of glass and silverware.

'You'll be fine,' he whispered, seating her before moving to his place. 'Mother always starts first anyway, so just take your cue from her.'

Indeed, the meal progressed well. The dishes were lavish and tasty. Christina was thoroughly enjoying herself. Lady McAlister and Rosemary proved delightful company and wonderfully enthusiastic conversationalists.

'So you are a minister's daughter from Dorset, my dear,' Lady McAlister said. 'How do you think you will find Bath society?'

'I do love parties,' Christina confessed in her light West Country lilt Jonathan found enchanting.

'And are not the officers so handsome and engaging?' Rosemary gushed.

'They do not look so dashing with seventeen inches of French steel sticking from their gizzards, lying in a pool of blood and gore and left to die on the battlefield,' Christina declared, aided by the champagne.

Silence!

Lady McAlister's fork froze inches from her lips, her eyebrows arching to the base of her tiara. Battlefield carnage was not usually a lady's topic of small talk at a Regency dining table.

'It is probably time I told you how Christina and I met,' Jonathan offered, showing no sign of embarrassment, in fact mildly amused by the evening's developments.

And so he did, with Christina filling in some details.

'And who says love does not blossom in adversity,' Lady McAlister said. 'What a charming story, you are such a brave girl. Thank you for saving Jonathan's life…and sharing his future. I don't know that I would have coped at all.'

'This from the lass who stood beside me loading muskets while we beat off a gang of rebels and their Indian allies in the Virginia Colony during the Revolutionary War,' Sir Monroe chuckled.

'The barrack room language took some getting used to,' Christina admitted.

'But how did Barnaby Grogan come to name your little girl?' Rosemary asked reasonably and Christina smiled.

'That was the name of his ship,' she replied.

'But a beautiful and true name in any event,' Lady McAlister declared.

'Dear Christina, I know I shall love you dearly and Bath's all very well, but however will you manage the London Season?' Rosemary wailed. She was a girl who knew her priorities.

'Oh, I think you will do very well, my dear,' Lady McAlister assured Christina, gently squeezing her hand. 'Very well indeed.'

'Cleric's daughter, soldier's wife, almost a sergeant's woman, and now an officer's lady — Yes, Lady McAlister, I believe I can handle London.'

'Calling me Mama will be good start.'

They retired late. Christina had dreaded the thought of meeting Jonathan's relations, but they turned out to be friendly, warm and genuinely pleased to have her join their family. Perhaps Sir Monroe and Lady McAlister's time in the colonies had made them more tolerant and worldly.

'Well, my darling,' Jonathan whispered as they snuggled under the bed covers, 'you see there was nothing to fear. I knew it would go well.'

'You remembered our story remarkably well,' Christina conceded, 'considering you were delirious most of the time.'

'Yes,' he agreed, 'it certainly was a bit blurry there for a while.'

'And of course, no one must ever know the true ending, must they?' Christina admonished.

'Jack Newell's secret is buried with him forever.'

'We've certainly had an interesting few months,' Christina said as she held Jonathan in their huge bed at Glen Briar Hall.

'I hope you won't find London society frivolous and boring,' he said.

'From what Rosemary tells me, it may be more dangerous than facing a French column.'

'I'm not really looking forward to the social season. I'd rather stay here and enjoy a country squire's life.'

'I'm sure we'll be up to it, and you'll enjoy being here all the more when we return.'

But as it turned out Christina's confidence was never tested. A few days later Major Jamieson rode up with a satchel filled with despatches.

Jamieson was shown into the drawing room where he met Jonathan.

'I thought you were still in Portugal, sir,' Jonathan said.

'Indeed I shall return directly, but Sir Rodney has charged me with some administrative tasks to tidy up — one of which is you.'

'I explained to their lordships, sir, but they have sort of left me in limbo.'

'I agree. From the look of that leg, we can only use you as an administrator, which is a waste as you were showing promise as a line officer, even if a little unconventionally.'

'They suggested I resign and sell my commission, sir.'

'So I believe. That is one option, but I can offer another.'

Jonathan said nothing.

'Have you considered the colonies?'

'India, sir?'

'You could seek a position in the Indian Army of course, but there is an opening for a captain with the New South Wales Corps at Sydney Town. A young fellow called John Macarthur got into a spot of bother during the Rum Rebellion a few years ago and it is high time he was replaced. As an inducement, the post includes a field promotion, which will save you the cost of buying your captaincy.'

'And my wife, sir..?' Jonathan ventured.

'Ah yes, that is another matter that did not well please Sir Rodney. No he was not well pleased at all. The colonel requires his subalterns to seek his permission to wed although he prefers them to remain single and not be distracted from their duty. As for marrying a private soldier's widow…'

Jamieson shrugged, but Jonathan was left in no doubt he had committed a gross military faux pas. Sir Monroe and Lady Abigail may not have qualms, but army snobbery was systemic and inbred. However, the colonial community with its criminal element appeared to hold no such prejudices.

'Take her with you by all means, McAlister. Your father found fortune and success in the colonies. Perhaps you will do likewise.'

'I must discuss the matter with Mrs McAlister, sir.'

'Then do so, but make haste. I will have your reply before I leave for Yeovil Barracks. Your ship sails within the month.'

Christina was actually thrilled as the thought of London society secretly *did* terrify her. Sir Monroe was enthusiastic too because he'd already met John McArthur who'd been banished from New South Wales, returning to England and resigning his commission to avoid a court-martial. Jonathan's father was already hatching out a lucrative scheme to invest in Merino wool and what better way to keep an eye on things than have his son right where the action was.

In September 1810 a sturdy brig set sail from Tilbury Docks bound for Port Jackson. So began the Australian branch of the McAlister Line…

The End

The Author

Richard Marman was born in Swindon, UK. His father was a RAF pilot who had served with distinction during WWII. His family moved from base to base after the war, including four years in Germany. They immigrated to Fremantle in 1962. Richard attended six primary and three secondary schools, so he is familiar with the 'new kid on the block' status.

After school, Richard joined the Royal Australian Air Force and trained as a pilot. He served for nine years, including a tour in Vietnam and a significant time flying in New Guinea. In 1975 Richard left the RAAF to fly with Ansett Airlines until the company closed in 2001 at which time he was a Boeing 767 captain. Afterwards he trained Singapore Airlines cadets on Lear Jets until 2007.

Leaving aviation behind, Richard completed a Diploma of Visual Arts at Tewantin TAFE and a Bachelor of Arts at the University of the Sunshine Coast, majoring in creative writing and graphic design. Many of Richard's book ideas have stemmed from University projects.

Richard lives on Queensland's Sunshine Coast with his wife Judy. They have twin daughters living interstate.

For more information visit:

www.richardmarman.com and www.richardmarman.net

The McAlister Line Reader Reviews

'...Masterfully handled and quite eloquent...wonderful.'

'I like this book [McAlister's Way] it covers issues that need to be addressed.'

'Waiting for the sequel'

'*McAlister's Spark* is a fast-paced, action-riddled amazing read you will struggle to put down.'

'A great action read for teenagers and great graphics...a great literary effort.'

'...with pirates and secrets set amongst the northern tropics, you're in for a delightful read. With a good sense of place and the voice to the detail it's [*McAlister's Way*] a very fast-moving action story that will have you wanting more.'

'*McAlister's Way* is a fast-paced, page-turning read — the kind of read where you lose track of time. Absolutely enveloping! Highly recommended!!'

'Through the non-stop action and the integration of history, new cultures and wars the reader is kept engaged from beginning to end on a literary roller coaster ride they won't soon forget.'

Wave and Web Series

Illustrated for Rita Hayward   **Illustrated for Elle Burton**

The dreaded dragon, Brimstone is terrorising the sleepy village of Oak Tree, so it's up to Prince Roger and his sister Princess Crystal to hunt down the fiery beast.

They are aided and hindered — as the case may be — by an evil knight, a mysterious good-guy, the local sheriff, loyal men-at-arms, forest brigands, a pair of trusty — and not so trusty — chargers, ogres, trolls and Oak Tree's citizens with a bunch of attitude.

There are thrills, spills, romance and a heap of rollicking good fun to be had by all.

McAlister
and the
Great War
Richard Marman

RICHARD
MARMAN
THE
WEALTH